I Made

A DEAL

WITH THE DEVIL

I MADE A DEAL WITH THE DEVIL
WITH THE DEVIL
(vol 1)

KAZ ZEN

for my little fighter,

CHAPTER 1

"Blood is thicker than water" had always been Evangeline Young's unspoken mantra—until those very words turned against her when the family she devoted her life to cast her away just because they found out she didn't share their blood. *What a ridiculous joke!*

Stepping on the brake, Eva rushed out of her car and made her way to her fiancé's penthouse. Julian hadn't been answering her calls.

When the elevator dinged and the doors slid open, she hurried out and briskly walked toward the unit located at the far end of the hallway. The sound of her classic black leather pumps echoed in the silence.

She tapped in the password in haste and opened the door.

As she stepped inside, she was about to call Julian's name when her eyes fell on a pair of red high heels lying on the floor.

Her whole world screeched to a stop.

After what felt like a very long pause, Eva forced her feet to move. Her heartbeat began to thud louder and louder the closer she got to the door to Julian's room.

Scandalous sounds reached her ears, and her heart stopped.

She stood there, unable to move. She came here to have someone to talk to, at least until the fire of her rage toward her grandfather calmed even a little. Just some solace was all she needed right now to make sure she wouldn't do anything rash that could worsen her situation. But gods... was the universe hellbent on destroying her to smithereens today? What did she do to deserve this?

Clenching her trembling hands, Eva tried to regulate her breathing. She took long deep breaths until her fists finally loosened up.

She stared at the door handle and slowly lifted her hand to hold it.

Then, with all the rage blazing within her, the door opened with a bang.

And there they were... two naked people on the bed. Fucking.

A numbness crawled through her.

Julian climbed off the bed, cursing. The woman under him also looked up, and Eva's face paled as if she had seen a ghost. Because the woman her fiancé was fucking was none other than her younger sister, Jessa Young.

Julian wasn't just Eva's fiancé; he was the man she had genuinely admired since college. They had been in a

2

relationship for almost a decade. Throughout their years together, Julian has always been kind and considerate. His consistent gentleness made Eva feel incredibly fortunate to have found a man like him.

Although their physical intimacy was limited to the occasional kiss, Eva never viewed this as a problem. It was because Julian had reassured her that he didn't mind the lack of sexual intimacy and was more than willing to wait until their wedding. He told her that this arrangement allowed them both to focus on building their careers.

He also expressed concern about distracting her or risking an unintended pregnancy. And Eva believed him wholeheartedly. She, too, thought their arrangement was ideal because the idea of pregnancy frightened her, knowing that precautions could still fail. So, she was so grateful that Julian understood their situation and priorities.

She had believed Julian was as comfortable with a sexless relationship as she was. She thought he was like her—just too busy to even think about sex.

But now, here he was…

What in the world is going on? Am I in a stupid soap opera dream right now?!

"What the fuck, Eva?! What are you doing here, barging into my home like this?" Julian roared.

Eva did not speak. She couldn't. This was the first time he had ever spoken to her so loudly. The first time he had looked at her with such scorn in his eyes. *Is this… is this really the Julian I know?*

3

He was the one who told her to come to his apartment whenever she needed him. The day he gave her his password years ago, he told her to come anytime without needing to inform him beforehand. He even told her during her first visit that she didn't need to ring the doorbell and should just enter, treating the apartment as hers. She remembered it clearly, just as she remembered those passwords, even though she hadn't visited his home more than a few times over the years.

Completely naked, he strode forward. His tall figure towered over her.

He leaned in closer.

The chocolate brown eyes she once adored now looked so cold, like frozen mud.

"We're over, Eva," he whispered. "I heard the news."

He pulled back. "Our shitty engagement is already over, so don't you ever show that ugly face of yours in front of me again. I've been sick of it for many years."

Eva couldn't believe what she was hearing. She had been in a relationship with this man for almost a decade! He had never once called her ugly. And he never once hurt her or made her cry. He had never once…

She clenched her fists so tightly that her nails threatened to pierce her skin. So, had he been acting all these years? Was everything, including the very person he had shown her since they were students, just an act all along? Did he ever actually like her, even a little?

Her eyes burned hot, but she held back her tears.

No. Don't you dare cry, Eva! I am not going to shed any tears in front of this asshole. Never. I would rather die than do that!

Steeling herself, she lifted her downcast eyes to look straight into his.

"Oh… is that so?" She somehow managed a sarcastic smirk. "Listen to me, Julian, and listen well. One day, I will make sure that you will die from utter regret. I promise you that. Just you wait."

And before Julian could react, Eva turned and slammed the door shut right in his face.

Eva leaned her head back against the headrest and closed her eyes.

After her breathing calmed a little, she revved the engine and stepped on the accelerator, sending her car speeding away from the place she never wanted to step foot in again.

The scene she had just witnessed kept replaying in her head. Julian's words echoed in her ears.

Her grandfather's cold and condemning expression also flashed in her mind. Then came a memory of herself when she was a little girl, watching her parents shower her sister with love while she stood in the corner, holding her perfect-score test papers.

She couldn't quite remember what she felt at that moment anymore, but she recalled slipping away silently, going back to her room, and hitting the books until she dozed off at her desk.

She had been raised to believe that Jessa deserved all the love and pampering not only because she was the little sister, but because Jessa wasn't expected to run the family company in the future.

Therefore, Eva genuinely believed it was fine for Jessa to live like a princess while she focused on studying and preparing herself for the very important responsibility she would one day inherit.

Eva's future had always seemed set. At least, that was what she had believed all her life. And she was totally fine with it.

In fact, she felt like studying and working were just perfect for her. Maybe it was because she was naturally wired as a studious and determined child, always focused on the future she envisioned for herself. The rigorous training and endless studying she endured from a young age never made her think of quitting or running away.

She never hated her family for sending her all the way to Europe to study when she was so young. She didn't resent them when they missed her graduation ceremonies or failed to even greet her on her birthdays.

She always told herself to understand that they were just too busy, and she barely had any time to spare either.

She had long accepted that this was simply how their family operated, that all these things were just normal for a family like hers.

She was totally fine with Julian being the only one to greet her on her birthday, a day she sometimes forgot herself. She was totally fine… despite everything.

But now… everything was crumbling into pieces.

Why did everything turn out this way? How could all of them do this to me?

Her mind continued screaming and hoping for a release, someway or somehow.

As she reached her favorite highway, Eva gritted her teeth. The road she loved for its view of the towering skyscrapers of the city-state she adored still looked as beautiful and vibrant as always.

Whenever she needed a breather, she would drive here, and every time, she felt comforted. She would always zoom in on one of the tallest skyscrapers, the XY Corporation headquarters, and feel revitalized.

But now, not even the vibrance of the view could make her feel even a little better. The familiar sight that once brought her pride now felt cold and distant. The headquarters of XY Corporation, once a symbol of her hard-earned achievements, hard work, and ambitions, no longer looked comforting.

Now… it just stood there… tall and gleaming and completely indifferent.

She jammed both her feet on the brakes.

Her car screeched to a halt in front of a bar along the highway.

Its name, Devil's Den, glowed invitingly in the night.

7

Eva desperately drew in deep breaths. Her breathing was short and labored, and the lack of oxygen reaching her brain caused her vision to swim dangerously. She knew she had to calm down. She needed to calm down!

After regulating her breathing and getting herself under control, Eva grabbed her small mirror. No matter what state she was in at the moment, she never wanted to look pitiful in front of anyone.

But the moment she saw her reflection, Julian's words echoed in her mind again. "Don't ever show that ugly face of yours in front of me ever again!"

Eva couldn't help but smile bitterly as she looked at herself. She grew up not caring that much about her physical appearance. All that mattered to her was knowledge, her goal, and her job. As long as there was no dirt, tears, or any sign of emotional weakness on her face, nothing else mattered to her.

She never thought she was pretty, but right now, she was finally seeing how ugly she really looked. Her skin was so dry, and her face was covered with pimple scars. She had dark circles, and her eye bags were so awfully puffy.

Her bitter smile faded as she wondered if things might be a little different if she did not look like this. But she quickly shook her head, throwing all those thoughts away, thinking nothing would've changed at all.

Desperate to completely stop the thoughts that were threatening to drown her, she took her thick round glasses off and cleaned them. She glanced at her red hair and sighed in relief that she had always kept it tied in a very tight bun. It was the only thing in perfect condition right now.

She stepped out of her car and entered the bar.

The Devil's Den seemed to be just another normal bar that many people visited. From the outside, it had a contemporary facade with large glass windows. Inside, the atmosphere was chic and upscale. The bar itself was a long, polished granite countertop with high-backed stools, illuminated by trendy pendant lights hanging from the ceiling.

Sweeping her eyes to the people inside, she immediately felt how out of place she was. She was dressed in her usual business attire—a white blouse, gray blazer, and a mid-calf skirt. Her PA told her many times she looked like an old, strict school principal, but Eva didn't care. She liked her usual business attire because to her, it was the most comfortable outfit.

Shaking her head, she tore her gaze from the ladies around her and leaned against the counter, ordering a drink with a request for it to be extra strong.

When her order came, she didn't wait a moment and took a sip. She winced at the taste of the alcohol as it burned a fiery trail down her throat.

"It seems that this is your first time drinking strong alcohol, eh, miss? Would you prefer to order something milder that most ladies drink instead? I can whip it up for you quickly," the bartender offered kindly.

Eva smiled wryly at the bartender's offer.

9

"No, thanks. I'm all right. This drink is fine. Anyway, I am here to drink to my heart's content for the first time in my life tonight!" She forced a laugh as she thought about how truly funny her life had suddenly become.

Once the bartender shifted his attention to another customer, Eva snorted mockingly at herself before she gulped her drink down in one go.

After a while, she signaled for the bartender to hit her with another glass of the same drink.

Soon, her eyes became a little unfocused, and she started conversing with her glass.

"Now look at you." She pointed emphatically at the innocent glass sitting before her. "You have worked so hard for so many years. You have never experienced these kinds of things." She glanced at the ladies recklessly dancing on the dance floor like they had no problems whatsoever in their lives.

"All these normal things people usually enjoy," she added before she returned her gaze to her glass and continued scolding it. "Why? Because all you thought and cared about your entire life up until now was that damned company, which you thought was going to be yours forever. You never had a normal childhood or adolescence… all because of your ridiculous dedication to earn as many degrees as possible, just so you could please and hope to impress your so-called family. And then you worked your ass off, giving your all. For what? Just to save the damn company? Poor you. You even went to the extent of sleeping in your office countless nights all alone. You never had the time to pay attention or care for yourself, and now look at you—nobody values or cares about anything that you have done. Now, your so-called family, who never actually considered you as their own, even stripped your hard-earned position away so their beloved daughter can now take over. Even your fiancé threw you away. He must have thought of you as just some toy. Haha. What a dramatic, stupid life you have, Evangeline Yo—" She paused. Her self-mocking smile faded before she gulped down another mouthful of her drink.

"That's right, you're not actually a Young," she continued talking to the glass. "You are not even related to them by blood! They never really considered you part of their family. You were just a pawn for them all along. Keep that in mind from now on. Make them all pay for casting you away and treating you like some slave they could easily throw away whenever they wanted once they were done using you! Make them regret it!" She slammed her fists on the counter. "All of them!"

"And how are you going to make them regret what they did to you?" a deep and mellow voice echoed.

Eva's head snapped to her right, and there she saw a man sitting next to her, looking so utterly handsome in a black suit. He was not looking directly at her but kept staring at his own glass.

Even in her drunken state, she couldn't ignore how even his side profile was breathtaking.

11

"Do you have enough money and power to bring them all down?" The man finally glanced over at her. She was momentarily struck. His eyes were as beautiful as a starry night, framed with enviable thick lashes. And his face... just seemed too gorgeous to be real!

Eva shook her head, and instead of gaping at the handsome-as-hell creature, she frowned at him.

"I-I," she stammered, and all of a sudden, she jumped from her seat and grabbed onto the man's collar. "I don't have enough money or power right now, but I will definitely find a way to bring them all to their knees! I'll make them all beg!" she hissed, shaking with anger.

"I will do everything, anything, to make them all regret what they have done, even if I have to sell my soul to the devil!" she added with dark rage burning in her striking blue eyes.

The man smirked.

He lifted his fingers and tucked some errant strands of her slightly mussed-up red hair behind her ear. "Be careful what you wish for, miss. A certain devil here might fulfill your wish and claim your soul in exchange."

"If that devil is here, do introduce him to me, handsome. I would like to make a deal with him," Eva drawled, smirking back at him.

CHAPTER 2

The man let out a brief sexy chuckle.

"How brave, but I guess it's because you're drunk right now. You might want to wait until you are more sober, miss."

His eyes then gleamed with wicked delight. "Because once I introduce him to you, there will be no turning back. It would be too late to regret."

"I am not drunk! Where is he? Tell me. And don't worry—even if he asks me to go to hell with him, I'll gladly follow. As long as he can give me all that I want."

The man only smiled. But in one swift movement, he stood and towered over her.

Leaning over her face, he pinched her chin gently and tilted her face up to his before his deep and sexy voice echoed in her ears. "All right, your wish is my command. I will gladly introduce you to him."

And with that, the man led her out of the bar.

13

But once they were at the car park, Eva frowned at the man.

"Where's the devil?" She pointed at her car. "You said that you're going to bring me to meet with the devil. Are you telling me that this car of mine is the devil?"

The gorgeous man chuckled quietly again, as if he found her reaction and her words somehow amusing.

"How adorable," he mumbled.

"You… you're…! Are you trying to fool me here—"

"I am not, miss." His smile faded as he looked at her with a serious expression. "It's just that the devil has told me previously that he does not like talking to anyone who is drunk. And you, miss, are so drunk that I bet you can't spell your own name forward, much less backward. So, I am going to send you home for now. Don't worry… I will introduce him to you myself the moment you're nice and sober."

"I told you I am not drunk!" Her voice became loud. "I. Am. Not. Drunk!"

She wobbled, but he stepped forward to catch and support her.

"Careful… What's your home address? Or is there anyone I can call to pick you up?" the man asked.

"Anyone to call…?" she echoed tonelessly. After a few seconds of blanking out, she smiled bitterly before scoffing.

"I don't want to go home. And there is no one… no one I can call." She bit her lip, then took in a steadying breath.

Suddenly, she grabbed his arm and dragged him toward her car.

"Don't think that you can go around wasting my time here as well. Oh… and I don't think it's wise for me to drive, so you drive." She pushed him down into the driver's seat, then she walked around and sluggishly lowered herself into the passenger's before propping her head tiredly against the headrest.

"All right, now drive," she commanded like a boss as she closed her eyes.

But the man did not start the car.

Eva opened her eyes and turned to him. "Why are you not starting the car? What are you still waiting for?" She narrowed her eyes at him. "Could it be that you're waiting for a bribe? Fine, fine!"

She grabbed her purse, but after rummaging around, she found that she had no cash on hand.

"Oh damn," she cursed.

At that very moment, a couple bumped into the front of her car.

Eva's gaze immediately fell toward two people cuddling, leaning against the car. The woman was kissing the man's neck, and then Eva watched the woman bite him.

When the man lifted the woman who just bit him into another blue car next to hers, her eyes narrowed.

She did not take her eyes off the blue car as it accelerated out of the car park.

Eva whipped her head toward the man next to her.

He was simply staring at her as if enjoying his time doing just that.

Eva suddenly crawled toward him.

His thick, dark brow lifted.

"Since I have no money right now, I guess this should be enough," she said nonchalantly.

And without warning, she lowered her head and kissed his neck, copying the exact same thing the woman earlier had done.

"Mm… you smell so good." Eva blurted out.

"You must stop that now, miss. Or else you will regret—"

She bit him. Hard.

A deep, rumbling sound came from him.

And just as she was about to kiss him again, she jerked. Her hands clamped over her mouth.

"Are you—"

His words were cut off by the retching sounds of her throwing up on his chest.

CHAPTER 3

Eva woke up in an unfamiliar room—a room that could only be described as luxurious.

Those high ceilings… those tall windows… and those heavy and regal draperies… *I am definitely dreaming, right?* she asked herself.

Most likely, unless you've been magically transported in one of the luxury castles in France, her inner demoness replied.

She swept her eyes to the burgundy damask wallpaper covering the walls, the polished hardwood floor, and the crystal chandelier hanging from the ceiling. Everywhere she looked, it only made the lines between her brows crease deeper.

"Where am I? What's with this extravagant room? Am I really dreaming?" she muttered out loud this time as she sat up.

And suddenly, memories from the previous night came rushing back. She remembered entering a bar and

17

meeting a man—a man so handsome she thought he definitely could only exist in dreams.

But… wait…

She pinched herself and felt the sharp sting of pain.

Her eyes slowly widened.

"Oh my God!" She frantically checked herself, taking stock of how she felt overall. She was still wearing her business suit and did not feel that her body was any different from usual. It was only her shoes and blazer that were not on her!

After a quick scan, she saw the missing items neatly arranged on a chair beside the bed. Her glasses were there too.

A long sigh of relief escaped her lips.

"Nothing happened to me, right?"

As she checked herself over again, she noticed that her long, voluptuous red hair was down.

"Did that handsome man bring me here?" Groaning, she buried her face in her palms.

"Oh my God, Eva… what have you gotten yourself into!"

She finally rose from the bed, grabbed her shoes and jacket, and put on her glasses.

Barefooted, she stepped out of the room.

"Am I inside an ancient château?" she could only mutter as she descended a grand staircase. "Marble steps… bronze handrails, chandeliers, ballrooms… this is definitely a house built in the 1800s!"

The place was massive and lavishly furnished. Every single thing was worth a considerable sum.

When she reached the ground floor, she saw a gigantic fireplace with an exquisite marble mantle and mirrored panels. "That's one wicked fireplace!"

She continued looking around, but the realization that she couldn't see anyone inside this huge place instantly made her feel mystified.

It wouldn't be surprising if it were deep in the night or dawn, but it was a busy time in the morning and she couldn't spot even a single maid around?

Thankfully, despite the emptiness, she didn't feel any dread. Maybe because the place was well-lit, luxuriously beautiful, and didn't feel eerie at all. But she didn't dare let her guard down. *Who knows what's hiding behind all these luxuries?*

Spotting the massive double doors, which she believed were definitely the entrance, Eva rushed toward them.

And once she was close, she realized how imposing they were. The doors stood approximately 12 feet high and 6 feet wide!

Without wasting a moment, she reached out, and the instant she touched the bronze door handle, a male voice echoed.

"Escaping already, little kitten?"

She froze.

The voice was deep, so deep it seemed to caress her skin like velvet.

Skin covered with goosebumps, Eva whipped around toward the owner of that darkly enticing voice. It was the beautiful man she had met at the bar!

Now that she was looking at him soberly, she couldn't believe that he looked even more handsome.

She had honestly thought that the gorgeousness she saw last night was distorted to perfection by her drunken mind.

But now here he was… wearing a dark robe, his short, damp, dark hair tousled, languidly holding a glass of wine in his hand as he stood there in the middle of such luxury.

The more she stared at him in that moment, the more she doubted if she was really not inside a dream. It was because the man was simply unreal, and this setting only intensified her feeling that the scene was too dramatically beautiful and unrealistic to be real.

"You… where am I?" she eventually demanded, trying to hide the fact that her heart was thumping wildly in its cage.

He smiled. A devilish smile.

"In hell, darling."

She was momentarily struck by that smile, but the words that came out of his lips made her shut her eyes and take a deep breath.

"Please be serious."

"Did you not tell me you wished to meet the devil?"

Eva could no longer help but glare at him aggressively. She did not have time for this!

But in that very moment, the memory of grabbing this man's collar and her declaration to meet the devil filled her mind.

She face-palmed. She could barely hold in the groan that was threatening to escape her lips.

Ugh… how embarrassing!

He walked closer to her, and then his forefinger was suddenly pressing gently but firmly on the lines gathered between her brows.

"Easy there, Pet," his voice sounded out, and Eva could only stand there, looking up at him.

She hadn't realized how tall he was until now. He was so tall he literally loomed over her! She thought she was used to tall men due to Julian's height, but this man… *he's definitely more than 6'5' tall!*

Despite their crazy size difference, she caught his wrist and glared at him.

"Don't call me that. I'm not your pet!"

He chuckled, and damn him again for also having the most pleasing male chuckle she'd ever heard.

"You are being too serious, Pet. Loosen up a bit—"

She flung his wrist aside.

"I'm leaving. Thank you, and sorry for the trouble I caused," she said seriously and turned to leave.

His palm suddenly pressed against the door right before her face.

That one move made her heartbeat drum wild. She could feel his nearness right behind her.

21

She felt him bend, and then he whispered in her ear. "If you think a simple thank you and sorry is enough for me... then I will forward you my apologies. Sorry to disappoint you, little kitten, but this devil won't be satisfied with that alone. Especially not after all the things that you did."

Eva swallowed.

Huh? Wait... things I did? What did I do?

"It seems you've yet to remember what you did, hm? Fine, then. I guess I'll have to show you some evidence to convince you that I am not simply making things up."

"E-evidence?" Eva stammered. *He has some kind of evidence against me?!*

"Here's the evidence, Pet."

Reluctantly, Eva turned around and saw him pulling on the ties that kept his robe closed. The sheer sight of him doing that slow movement made blood rush to her face.

Wait... is he actually going to strip right in front of me? Is he some kind of godly pervert?!

The long black robe fell open, and Eva almost gasped in relief when she saw he was only half-naked underneath.

"Right here, little kitten." His voice pulled her attention away from the most perfect abs she'd ever seen.

Her eyes were back on his face, and she saw him smiling like a mischievous devil.

"Here." His long, veiny finger pointed at two very obvious marks—one hickey and one bite mark— decorating his neck.

Eva's lips parted, and then she finally remembered the rest of the events from last night. That she had literally pushed him inside her car and even kissed and bit his neck without asking for permission! *Oh, goodness! Now you've really gone and done it, Eva!*

She couldn't believe she could be that bold when drunk.

It was not like this was her first time ever drinking alcohol. But she had never let herself get so inebriated before. She was all about self-control and discipline. She had seen too many people who had gotten themselves smashed and ended up embarrassing themselves big time. And since she was the kind of woman who was always so uptight and cared so much about her reputation, she had always put herself under her own very strict surveillance.

But here she was now. *My God!*

When she returned her gaze to him, he was still smiling. For some reason, his wicked mouth that had curled at the sides was making her nervous. But she kept her composure. What should she do? Honestly, she wasn't confident that this man wanted an apology. She felt like... he wanted something else.

She was about to ask him how much money he wanted when her eyes once again looked around the house, which was screaming with luxury.

Did a man living in such luxurious comfort even need money? But what if he was not the one who owned this house? But... he looked...

Before she realized it, her eyes traveled over him from head to toe.

Why the hell did she have the feeling that he was some kind of high-ranking aristocrat?!

Eva had met a few aristocrats in the past, and although she had not had the opportunity to meet kings and queens, she had met her share of princes and other bluebloods. This was how she had an idea of the kind of air surrounding them. And she was surprised to find that this man had an even stronger presence than all those she had met before. Who was this man? Or were her senses playing a trick on her?

"Who are you?" Eva finally asked.

"Who am I…" his deep voice drawled. "How about you guess, hm?"

Eva creased her brows. "I don't have time to play a guessing game with you."

"That's a shame then." He just smiled.

It was strange how he seemed to be so tolerant of her uptight attitude. Most people, be they men or women, could not wait to end a conversation with her, except when the conversation revolved purely around business. So why did this man sound like he was trying to drag their conversation out?

"If you keep beating around the bush, I'm leaving."

"All right," he said, staring at her, his wicked smile fading.

"I am the devil."

Silence reigned between them for a moment. It was so quiet that an invisible crow might as well be seen flying and cawing over their heads.

And then her imagination kicked into high gear, and she could very well imagine him with horns and a tail.

She slapped her forehead with her palm, and then her expression abruptly returned to her usual businesslike face.

"If you are not taking me seriously, just let me leave please," she snapped.

But the man simply sipped at his wine with such grace. His intense gaze, shooting at her right over the rim of his glass, was simply… mesmerizing.

And before she knew it, she was watching his Adam's apple bob up and down as he swallowed his drink. This man… how could a man exude such overflowing sexiness and grace just by drinking damn wine?!

Eva shook her head to clear her mind. *My God, this man is truly dangerous!* This was definitely a man every woman must be careful with!

Just as she was thinking to herself, she felt his fingertip lightly brush over the skin between her brows again as if to smoothen the deep lines that were furrowing there.

"This line here will truly become permanent if you keep frowning so hard like this," he said, and Eva roughly caught his wrist once more.

"And whose fault is it that I am frowning? I'm saying it for the last time: if you're not taking me seriously, then just please let me leave."

25

"I am taking you very seriously, Pet."

Eva narrowed her eyes. Then she gave a small, very unladylike snort.

"You're saying that you telling me 'I am the devil' is you being very serious?" She emphasized the word "very" before sighing heavily and shaking her head. "I am not drunk anymore. So stop playing around with me. If you won't, then just let me leave. I told you I don't have time for games like this."

"All right, all right." He looked as though he had finally given in. The mischief in his eyes faded, and his expression finally became serious.

He stretched his hand out to her.

"Gage. I'm Gage Acheron."

Eva stared at his large, veiny hand. *Gage... Acheron... where have I heard that name before? Wait... Acheron?!*

That surname had her looking at him with shocked surprise.

Is he really an Acheron?!

The Acherons were the oldest and most influential old-money family in the entire city-state of Letran. *Could it be that this man is... no way... right?*

When she reasoned to herself that he might be a distant relative of the infamous family, the tension within her eased slightly. This man was definitely not an immediate family member because she heard there were only two immediate members of the Acheron family right now! It was only George Acheron, the chairman, and his grandchild, which was said to be a girl. There was also the possibility that he wasn't telling the truth and was just using that surname.

She took his hand.

"Eva. I'm Eva You—" She bit her lip. She was reminded of her current situation and everything that happened before she ended up in that bar.

She clenched her fists tight, then squared her shoulders, refusing to show any vulnerability in front of a complete stranger.

Her eyes became fierce as she looked him straight in the eyes. "Eva," she said firmly, leaving off her last name. "Just Eva."

His dark eyes seemed to soften, and thankfully, he didn't press her further about her full name. Instead, he nodded with a small smile. "Just Eva, then."

"Mr. Acheron. I am truly sorry for what I did to you. I was drunk and…"

The scene of that moment when she bit him flashed in her mind, and involuntarily, she blushed. But she quickly pushed the scene out of her thoughts. Clearing her throat, she added, "I know you don't look like someone who is in dire need of money. But money is all I have to pay you for the inconvenience I have caused."

He swirled the wine in his glass with an unsettlingly graceful motion.

Eva couldn't believe how something as simple as watching that red wine swirl in the glass could hold her seemingly spellbound. She felt like she was staring into a hypnotic spiral.

"Hmm. That would be problematic." His voice broke through her trance, smooth and rich.

Eva blinked, tearing her gaze away from the swirling wine to look at him.

"But since I am the victim here, don't you think I should be the one deciding what kind of compensation I want?" he continued.

"V-victim?" Eva stuttered a little.

Her eyes fell on the bite mark on his neck, and she could only berate herself inwardly once again.

"Mr. Achero—"

"Just Gage," he drawled. "No need to be formal with me."

"All right, Gage. What is it that you want?"

A slow smile curved across his lips. A smile looking so mischievous yet seductively hot.

Damn this man to hell! There is no need for you to smile like that!

Eva had met quite a number of good-looking men before. In her line of work, she had even met with a few top celebrities and other big personalities, and she was proud to say that she had built up quite a tolerance when it came to handsome guys. A few had tried to seduce her, young men who were obviously not into her but were just desperate for rich and successful sugar mommies. And it may seem a little unbelievable but one sharp blade-like look from her, and the men never came back to bother her anymore.

But this man... She had been glaring at him for a while now; she even made a move to grab at his collar like she was some violent woman last night. Most men would definitely run away and ignore a woman like her because she knew that most men were suckers for soft, sweet, and delicate ladies. She, however, was far from soft, never sweet, and certainly not delicate... and that was probably one of the biggest reasons why Julian had thrown her away like trash now that she had nothing left to her name.

So why? Why was this man not throwing her out of his luxurious castle of house yet? Why was he still smiling at her as though he found her interesting? She knew she was never interesting as a woman! She also knew how ugly she was now! So, what was this guy really up to?

His... behavior must be due to some ulterior motive, right? Or maybe he is just bored, and that's why he's dragging this.

"I won't ask for much, Pet. I just want you to stay with me... in this house... until this bite mark and hickey disappear," he spoke leisurely, all the while still swirling the wine in his glass. "That shouldn't be all too hard to do, right?"

Eva blinked. Speechless.

W-what?

He wanted her to stay in this castle-like house with him until those marks on him disappeared. Wait... would that not take quite a long time?! Both the bite mark and

29

hickey, if left to heal on their own, would take up to two weeks. And from the little that she had interacted with this man, she just felt like he would definitely drag it out for the two weeks. That meant a whole fourteen days!

No… this man… he most definitely was joking around with her.

She stared at him with a serious gaze.

Right, I'm sure that anytime now, he is going to laugh the moment I fall for his joke!

She focused her gaze on him, observing his facial expressions closely as she waited for his laugh to erupt.

However, stare as she might, the laughter she expected did not come. He just stood there, looking at her with the same unchanging, calm expression. It was as though he was still waiting for her response.

What?! Is he really serious about that condition? He is not joking?!

Her lips parted, and her palms started getting a little damp as she felt nervousness running through her veins. She was utterly speechless. She had fully prepared herself to be slapped with some serious compensation for her slip-up, but he had just wanted her to…

Wait… wait a minute!

Eva's eyes slowly stretched wide at the thought that came to her.

There is no way… could it be that…

Her eyes narrowed, and her gaze sharpened into an accusing glare. A flash of contempt flickered in her eyes as she became almost certain that this man was keeping her here for that very reason.

But… no… that did not make any sense… just look at him…! Why would he even want an ugly woman like me?

Running his fingers through his hair with a somewhat offended half-smile on his face, Gage broke the silence. "If you think that I am asking you to stay that duration so you can serve me in bed, then I'm sorry to disappoint you, but you're wrong." His eyes lazily swept her form from head to foot.

Eva could only blush, embarrassed but not surprised that she was right. Of course… There was absolutely no way this man would bother with someone like her. If he wanted a woman, he could just make a call and goddesses would come flocking to him!

Clearing her throat, she averted her gaze and pretended to look around.

"So, you're saying that I just need to stay here until my bite marks on you disappear?" she echoed his earlier conditions as if she was still unable to believe it.

He nodded. "Correct. Because I'm in dire need of a companion right now."

Eva returned her gaze to him with a deadpan expression on her face.

Huh? This man… is he a kid in need of a companion just because he is home alone? Seriously?

"My maid has run away, and I need some time to look for a replacement. So, since you're already here, and you do need to compensate me, I guess this would be the most convenient arrangement I can come up with on such short notice," he said while nodding to himself, still looking very serious.

Eva could only stand there and look at him, talking to herself inwardly. *M-maid? So, he is actually planning on making me his temporary maid?*

"Any more questions, Miss Eva? Don't tell me that you are unsatisfied with my conditions. You're not going to tell me you would rather me bed you than have you stay with me and accompany me, are you..." He trailed off when she glared at him.

He flashed that devilish smile again.

"Fine," she bit out curtly, and immediately, within the safe confines of her mind, she cursed. *Goddammit! Why do I feel like this sly devil is tricking me? But... I do not really have a choice here, right? I have not seen anyone else inside this huge house aside from him. Could it be that he is really all alone and... All right, relax, Eva. Just calm down. No point in getting your panties in a bunch. Let us go with the flow for now and just stay alert. We can play it by ear.*

Somehow, her internal monologue helped calm her down somewhat.

"Good girl," he said, patting her head.

She shot him a sharp glare. "Don't 'good girl' me. I'm already a twenty-eight-year-old woman."

He chuckled. "Still a good girl for me," he murmured before removing his hand from her head.

"All right, so from this moment on, you're not allowed to leave this house until"—he pointed at the bite mark on his neck— "this thing here disappears."

He spun around, leaving Eva to gaze at his back as he walked ever so gracefully toward the fireplace. He plopped down on the cushion, crossing his long legs comfortably.

Eva bit on her lip as she began debating with herself inwardly again.

Damn. What the hell did I just get myself into? All this is just a coincidence and my awful luck for running into such a beautiful, weird man, right? Right?

She took a long, deep breath. This was the first time she had encountered a situation like this. She did not know how to deal with a man like this when her cold treatment and glares did not seem to ward him off.

"Come over here, Pet," his sexy voice echoed and pulled Eva's full attention back to him.

She walked toward him and halted when she realized she was already less than five steps away from him.

"What's wrong?" he asked.

"Don't you think I should go home first?" Eva replied quickly.

He tilted his head slightly. "Why?"

"Well, I don't have any clothes with me."

"I'll get someone to buy you everything you need for the time that you are here." He picked up his phone. And as soon as the call was connected, he continued speaking. "I need clothes for a woman."

"Wait… wait a moment." Eva was flabbergasted.

Lifting a brow at her, he moved the phone away from his ear. "Our bargain is already finalized. I said you couldn't leave this place until these marks disappeared. You agreed earlier. No reneging on your words, Eva."

Eva was about to retort again, but her head suddenly throbbed painfully.

"Now go back to that room you came from and take a shower to freshen up. I'll bring your clothes over in a few moments."

CHAPTER 4

A long, drawn-out sigh echoed out in the luxurious bathroom as soon as Eva turned the shower off.

It seemed she was really not dreaming after all. She had truly come across a devilishly handsome but mysterious and strange guy who wanted her to become his temporary maid!

Seriously… is it just me, or are these turn of events really becoming more and more fictional?

Another long, deep sigh escaped her lips as she swept back her palms over her hair.

Cleaning was easy for her. Though she was raised in a rich family, when she was in Europe, she always did her own chores. She could literally do anything.

Well, except cook deliciously. That was why that devil's condition was not a big deal to her… it was just that she had some trouble believing it. And she really could not quite figure out if he was just doing this for fun or if there

35

was some other agenda he was planning. The most frustrating thing was that she did not really have a choice right now.

She could not afford to make a mistake and create another problem. Especially because this man seemed really filthy rich.

"Alright… just calm down and find a way out of this," she whispered as she finally finished her bath.

Soon, she stepped out of the bathroom, and her eyes immediately fell onto the clothes that were already neatly laid out on the bed.

She lifted the pink-colored pajamas and glanced at the skin-colored bra and panties. The pajamas had small bears and ducklings printed all over.

Eva did not know what to say. When was the last time she had ever worn something so cute and childish?

Sighing, Eva hastily got dressed.

When she was finally back in the living room, Gage was still sitting in the same chair near the fireplace, but he was properly dressed now, wearing a crisp white shirt and black pants.

Thank God! His ridiculously perfect body was truly distracting!

But despite the fact that he was now fully clothed, he still managed to look as distracting as before. Shirtless or not! Damn this man!

Eva opened her mouth when her stomach decided to "speak up" first.

Silence.

Then another loud growl.

Her hands flew to cover her face. Her ears red-hot with embarrassment.

As she put down her hands and was about to speak to cover the rumbling sounds of her stomach, she was shocked at the sight of him suddenly appearing right before her, already squatting down.

Her eyes slowly stretched wide as she looked down at him and then at the pair of white slippers that he placed in front of her bare feet.

He looked up.

"Wear these," he said simply, and Eva could only blink at him.

What... what is he doing? Hadn't he asked me to stay as the replacement for his maid? Then why is he... acting like...

"Anything wrong?" His voice nearly jolted her out of her skin.

Snapping out of her daze, she cleared her throat.

"N-nothing," she replied, averting her gaze from him as she hastily slid her cold feet into the warm, fluffy slippers.

"All right, come along with me, Pet." He started walking, and she followed obediently behind him.

Eva's heart raced. She still couldn't believe what he had just done. It might be a mundane action, but to her, it was absolutely out of the ordinary. No one had ever done that for her before. She was certain that most men would never do that for a grown woman. Yet, here was this man, who looked absolutely perfect and wealthy as hell, squatting down right in front of her to make her put on a house slipper!

No... this is definitely not normal. What the hell is this man up to?

Her eyes narrowed suspiciously at him.

When she realized that he was leading her to the kitchen, something popped into her mind.

A mischievous smirk slowly tugged at the corner of her lips, and her eyes brimmed confidently.

"Alright, here's the chance you've been waiting for, Eva," she inwardly told herself. "Time for you to show him your nonexistent talent in cooking. I'm sure once this sly devil tastes your food, he will definitely throw you out. Easy escape!"

CHAPTER 5

Eva sat silently, drinking and suspiciously observing the man over the rim of her glass. When they had entered the kitchen earlier, to her utter dismay, the devil had not actually asked her to cook. Instead, he had even pulled out a chair for her, made her sit, and told her to watch.

When she attempted to stand and offer him some help, he ordered her to stay still and wait!

Pinching the skin between her brows, she narrowed her eyes at the now busy, handsome chef, feeling as though she was going to have another pounding headache.

No matter how much she thought about it, she couldn't come up with any logical reason why he was behaving this way. She was meant to be his maid, so why was she just sitting there like she was the master of the house instead of him?

Damn… this is not as easy as I thought!

Soon, a steaming bowl of soup was placed before her, and Eva salivated at the smell of the delicious-looking food.

When she lifted her eyes, he was sitting across from her, smiling.

"Go on, dig in. This will be good for your hangover," he said, resting his temple against his knuckles as if preparing to watch something very entertaining.

"You watched me like you were trying to solve an intricate puzzle the entire time I was cooking. I'm sure you would have seen it if I put something weird in there," he said when she didn't move and just stared at him suspiciously.

Eva cleared her throat before unceremoniously grabbing the utensils.

She scooped up a spoonful of soup and blew on it before sipping.

Oh, wow!

She felt her shoulder involuntarily relax.

"How is it?" he asked, looking so dazzling that Eva almost choked on her second mouthful.

"It's good," was all she could say.

Damn you! How can you cook so well, too? This is bad. I am hungry, and this is probably the most delicious chicken noodle soup I have ever tasted!

It was warm, with just the right hint of saltiness from the seasonings and sweetness from the vegetables. The flavors seemed so simple, so why did they taste so utterly delicious?

Before she realized it, she devoured and enjoyed the soup to the point that she had momentarily forgotten about his existence, until he pushed a plate of whole grain toast before her.

Finally jolted out of the soup heaven, she looked up at him and said with a sharp gaze, "You're not actually a male witch in disguise planning to fatten me up before eating me, are you?"

Gage threw his head back and laughed. Really laughed.

The sound of his laughter was just so... so good. It was so pleasing to Eva's ears that it sparked tingles in her auditory canals if that even made sense! Not only did the man cook yummy food, but even his laugh sounded so mouthwatering!

My God... this guy's really too good to be real, isn't he?!

Sneaking glances at him, Eva realized he was truly looking amused.

And before she knew it, her eyes just subconsciously fell on his thin, sinuous lips.

She quickly averted her eyes and looked elsewhere.

Damn this man to hell! Why does he have to look this handsome? I should be negotiating with him right now, not admiring his handsomeness like he's some Greek god! Get a hold of yourself, Eva!

Just as she was busy scolding herself, his voice pulled her attention back to him. "Hmm... What if I am indeed a male witch?"

He rested his head on his knuckles again as he stared at her, one eyebrow lifting.

"What are you going to do about it? Hm?"

41

Eva belatedly reddened with embarrassment as she finally realized how cringey the words she'd spouted earlier must have been.

Dammit! Why the hell did I even say that out loud? What's going on with me embarrassing myself like this?

Forcing herself to bounce back, she lifted her eyes to look at him, trying to keep her face as straight as possible, pretending she had not said anything embarrassing.

Clearing her throat, she spoke in a matter-of-fact tone. "Well, if you're indeed a male witch, I'd like you to help me find my phone. I can't remember where I left it."

"Ah, yes. Your phone." He casually slipped his hand into his pocket and pulled out the said phone before handing it to her. "I took it along with me when I saw it in the car a while ago."

Eva took the phone from him hesitantly.

After giving it a quick check, she turned the phone on. Immediately, it started pinging. Notifications for messages continued ringing one after another.

Eva creased her brows.

Just as she was about to open one of those messages, a call came through.

It was her secretary.

Eva stared at it for a few seconds, then looked at Gage. "Sorry, I need to pick this up."

"Go on," Gage replied casually.

Eva walked to a corner of the kitchen and swiped across her phone. "Yes, May? What is—"

"Oh my God, ma'am! You're finally answering your phone! Where are you? Did you see the news? The commotion it stirred up is insane!"

Eva frowned.

"Slow down, May. What do you mean by commotion? My phone was turned off the whole time, so I have yet to check any news."

"My God! Boss! I'm talking about your announcement! You even announced that you officially stepped down as CEO last night, effective immediately."

Eva froze.

And just like that, all the anger that she felt yesterday came back like tidal waves, crashing hard at her.

"I never made any announcement," Eva hissed. Her tone was cold and sharp, like blades that would draw blood from whomever it was directed. "I didn't step down! They…"

"I know, boss. But now rumors are already spreading that you submitted your resignation because you have been accused of fraud and misconduct! My God! I'm not sure of what to do anymore, ma'am! My phone is ringing off the hook from reporters trying to get an inside scoop on this. Where are you? Please tell me. I can come get you."

Eva's grip on her phone tightened until her knuckles turned white.

W-what? Fraud? Misconduct?!

She ended the call without answering her secretary and quickly browsed through the messages in her phone's inbox, skimming through all the texts asking her if the rumors were true.

Her fingers started to shake.

Her phone rang again, but she did not bother to answer it this time. The shaking became more violent until the phone fell from her grip.

Gage was suddenly there, picking up the phone on the floor.

Abruptly, Eva turned around and faced the wall, trying to hide her face from him.

"Please help me turn the phone off," she managed to say in a small voice.

After a few moments of silence, Gage spoke from behind her. "I have an unwanted visitor, Pet. You wait here. I'll be right back."

As soon as he left, Eva buried her face into her palms and screamed within her mind. *What?! Fraud? Misconduct?! Are you kidding me?! Why? Why must you go to this extent? How could you do this to me? Are you all really serious about destroying me completely? Why?!*

Slamming the side of her fist against the wall, Eva swore under her breath, "I will never forgive any one of you!" She gritted her teeth. "I swear, I will make you all pay tenfold!"

Overcome with anger, she walked out of the kitchen. She still did not know what to do or where to even begin. However, there was something she wanted to do right now, or else she swore she would totally lose it.

First things first, she must leave this house so she could go and start dealing with her situation! If she were to just stay here and wait around, she might end up exploding in anger! No! She refused to just let those scums do this to her!

Her steps were hurried as she stormed toward the living room, but the moment she saw Gage sitting leisurely and graciously in that same chair by the fireplace, she paused. Then her eyes were immediately drawn to a man handsomely dressed in black and wearing fine wire-framed glasses who was standing before Gage.

Eva's eyes widened as she recognized him.

Wait! Isn't that... Mr. Whitmore? That's the infamous secretary of Mr. George, the CEO of ACEON Conglomerates! What is he doing here?!

And before she had realized it, she had already hidden herself behind the wall.

"Sir, master sent me here to ask you one last time. If you're still not interested in taking the CEO position for ACEON, the chairman will give the position to someone else. He has already prepared a list of candidates to choose from," Mr. Whitmore informed Gage.

Eva was taken aback. What? Wait... this man... he's being offered the position as the next CEO of ACEON?

ACEON Conglomerates was a multinational, diversified company owned by the Acherons. It was based in the city-state of Letran but had a strong global presence with offices in major cities such as New York and Tokyo.

ACEON operated across a wide range of industries, including technology, healthcare, finance, energy, and consumer goods. And it was also XY's ultimate rival.

From the day she was appointed CEO of XY, she viewed ACEON as the formidable giant she had to conquer to reach the top. She worked tirelessly for years to achieve this goal, and finally, just this year, she managed to elevate XY to unprecedented heights, surpassing ACEON for the very first time.

Eva knew that part of XY's recent success was due to ACEON's internal struggles, where their CEOs kept resigning for unknown reasons. Despite this, she was immensely proud of her achievement. She knew how hard she had worked and believed that even though ACEON wasn't at its best, her efforts and the rise of XY under her leadership were undeniably valid and significant accomplishments.

"Hmm... CEO, huh? But that's a lot of work, Mr. Whitmore," Gage drawled out lazily, and to her surprise, Mr. Whitmore didn't seem shocked by Gage's nonchalant attitude.

"Oh, come on, sir." The secretary was patient, and it seemed like the man was already used to Gage's responses. "You're the one who made the company soar years ago. You and I both know you can handle this position easily. And as the heir, you can't just sit here and watch the company crumble, can you?"

Eva was stunned.

So this man wasn't just an Acheron—he was the heir?!

Everyone knew that George Acheron, the chairman and head of the Acheron family, had lost his only son many years ago. And the only immediate family he had now was his grandchild who has never been revealed publicly. Everyone thought the grandchild was a girl but it's actually not?! To think that this elusive grandchild was none other than this handsome but kind of strange man she'd met in the bar!

What kind of luck did she have to run across the heir of her longtime rival and end up in his house? She could never have imagined finding herself inside the mansion of the Acherons!

"I have already long since lost interest in this, Mr. Whitmore. You know that very well. If I become the CEO, I'll most probably cause the company to go bankrupt," Gage said casually. "Lack of motivation is a serious flaw, and you know you can't force that. The only thing I can gain from this is more money. But you and I both know how useless that is to me right now. Why would I want to work my ass off to earn more money when I already have more than what I can never even finish spending in this lifetime?"

The secretary sighed, defeated. "Er… well, the master just thought that maybe you're bored now and might want to work hard again?"

"Ah, I'd be bored to death if I actually took on that position, Mr. Whitmore."

47

Mr. Whitmore sighed again. "Al… All right, I understand, sir. I will forward your message to the master so he can start choosing from the list of candid—"

"Wait!" Eva's voice echoed in the spacious living room.

Mr. Whitmore whipped around, and his eyes widened at the sight of Eva.

Eva strode toward them. Her jaw was set, and her eyes were so intense.

Mr. Whitmore furrowed, and he blinked several times. And when recognition flickered in his eyes, he took a step back, nearly tripping over his own feet. "Miss Young?! W-w-what are you doing here?"

"She's my guest," Gage answered him.

Mr. Whitmore's lips parted slightly as his head darted from Eva to Gage and back again.

"Your guest? When did the two of you even…"

"Excuse me, Mr. Whitmore," Eva said. "Please let me borrow Gage. We'll be back in a while."

Before Mr. Whitmore could respond, Eva took Gage's hand and tugged him back toward the kitchen with a determined grip.

CHAPTER 6

"Are you... are you really going to reject that offer?" Eva asked, staring hard at Gage.

Gage flashed her a crooked smile.

"Let's just say... I'm pretty lazy," he replied, then winked playfully. "I don't have a plan to spend my bachelor life just sitting in a chair all day and even nights simply to make more money I don't even need."

Eva pinched the skin between her brows.

Arrogant devil!

Though she knew he was just probably being honest, she still couldn't help but want to...

Ugh! Why is life so unfair?

"Then hire me," she said.

Her blue eyes were blazing with nothing but confidence and unwavering will. "Hire me. You may not have any idea who I am, but I am the CEO—I mean, former CEO of XY Corporation. Hire me, and I promise to bring ACEON to the top again and crush XY in the process!"

"So... you're that female CEO who made XY overtake ACEON, huh?"

"Yes. That's me. So, hire me. I promise I can deliver what I say," Eva replied with conviction.

Gage rubbed his chin, his mystifying gaze scrutinizing her.

"I know the chairman and board will not accept me," Eva continued. "Even though I am the ex-CEO now, there is still no way that they would be willing to hire me, especially if they hear the rumors..." She paused for a moment.

"That's why you should accept the position and then hire me to do almost all the work for you since your reason is because you're lazy. All you have to do is appear here and there for some meetings and then cooperate with me in crushing XY Corp."

Gage hummed.

"You want to do all the work... and I assume you don't want to be credited?"

"Yes. I know this is fraudulent but..." She bit her lip, realizing the gravity of what she was trying to offer to him. She was literally offering him to commit a crime!

Gods... I am really just desperate right now, aren't I?

"So you don't mind at all if you won't be getting any recognition?" Somehow, the nonchalant way he talked, as if he didn't hear that one word she just uttered, made her feel like he didn't care about the morality of what she had just offered.

And before she knew it, her rage blazed within her, consuming all reasons.

"I don't care," she immediately responded. "I'm fine with it. All I want is to take revenge right now. I'll make them all regret what they did to me. I told you I would do anything to get back at them. I want them to feel the pain of losing something they treasure so much! And this is only the beginning."

Clenching her fists so hard, she stared at him with all the intensity she could muster. "I intend to fully pay them back for their wonderful 'care' of me with added interest!"

Gage kept his gaze on her, not saying a word.

"I am being very serious. I told you, even if I have to make a bargain with the devil, I'll do it."

"You did say that…"

"Yes. If that's what it takes."

"All right." Gage nodded, and a languid smile spread on his face. He leaned against the wall. His gaze remained fixated on her. "Let's make a deal then, Eva. I'll give it to you. All the things you want…"

He paused for a few moments.

"However… are you certain you're willing to do anything in exchange, hmm? Eva?"

Eva nodded furiously. "Yes! Anything!"

He smiled. Then he cocked his head and crossed his arms. "Are you really sure?" he asked again.

"I. Am. Sure. Mr. Acheron," she said firmly, stressing her reply word by word.

He suddenly bent to whisper in her ear. "How about... Gage darling?!"

"W-what are you...?" She could only stammer before sighing to regain her composure. "Will you please stop doing that? I am serious here... please stop throwing me off!"

"All right, looks like you're a bit relaxed now." He leaned against the wall again.

Just as Eva thought he'd finally gotten back to business, he rubbed his chin and uttered, "But 'Gage darling' sounds great, right?"

This... this man...

"All right." His voice and the look in his eyes finally became serious. "Then I'll be stating my price for the bargain."

Eva's heart began to race.

She knew that she had to expect the worst. She was well aware of how this world worked after all. If you want something big, pay something big. That was a given because the world simply worked that way.

As Gage parted his lips, Eva subconsciously held her breath.

"Marry me," he said.

Eva's mind screeched to a halt. Dumbfounded.

She could almost literally hear the tires screeching in her mind.

She blinked a few times before she managed a response. "Wha... What? Wait, wait! What? You... you're not trolling me, are you?" Of all the worst things she'd imagined, him asking her to marry him never even crossed her mind. *This isn't some soap opera! This is reality, so why the hell is he saying such nonsense? Can't this damn devil be serious for once?!*

"I'm serious, Eva."

Eva could only look at him in shock and disbelief. She could see the change in his eyes, and it seemed like he was truly serious!

"You... you really want to marry me? W-why?" she asked.

He tilted his head to the side a little. "Isn't the answer to that question obvious?"

"You... want a wife..."

"Need a wife."

"Is it because your old man is threatening that he won't give you your inheritance if you don't get married as soon as possible?" Eva blurted out. She knew that this kind of thing was very common in the upper classes of society. Many heirs were forced to get married by their family, and most of the time, these heirs could only opt for a marriage of convenience.

There was a short pause before he nodded subtly.

"But... why me? I mean, I'm just a stranger. Wait... you're just going to do this for a show, right? I mean, you're going to marry me and then divorce me after a set time has passed once you receive what you want, am I right?"

53

Her mind kept giving her ideas. Ideas she knew were very much possible. She was not ignorant about these things because she was aware that they truly happened in reality.

In the world of the wealthy, marriages of convenience or marriages with benefits were the norm, and love… She honestly did not know if that still mattered to them. She had seen and heard too much to doubt that.

So this was the only explanation she could think of for why this man would want to marry her—an unwanted nobody who did not have beauty or even status right now. Not to mention that her name was being ruined even further, even at this moment.

I guess he wants a useful woman like you? her inner demoness whispered in her ear. *You even offered to do all the company's work for him after all. And it seems he already knew that you're a very competitive person and have all the skills needed for that position.*

That makes sense. Or maybe… Eva thought to herself, *he chose me because he can easily discard me when he doesn't need me anymore. I guess he might have thought that I wouldn't be the type of woman who would cling to him. And maybe he thinks that I'm the type of woman who will sign the divorce papers without putting up any fight or complaints as long as I get my revenge.*

Eva stared at Gage so intently as she thought about all of that. Even though this man had not done anything bad to her, she would not be naive to think that he was doing this for any better reason.

"Are you… really sure? I mean… of choosing me as your wife?" Eva asked. Her heart was still in chaos right now, but in all honesty, she knew that this arrangement seemed to be more beneficial for her than for him. At least for now.

"Why? You think you're not worthy enough to be hitched to a handsome man like me?" he asked with a mischievous smirk.

"Of course not," Eva replied. "I honestly think that you'd be lucky to marry a woman like me." She lifted her chin as she said that, and Gage chuckled.

His indolent smile widened.

"Not bad, Pet. So that seems to be a yes."

"Wait a moment… don't you think we need to take a little more time to think over this? I mean… we should discuss our conditions first, right? Because I am certain you must have your own conditions. And I need to know them all before I… before I make the final decision."

"Smart girl. However, I need to tell Mr. Whitmore about my decision now. If I let him go without accepting the position—"

"No! Wait! I… can't you just go and accept it?"

Gage raised a brow.

"I can't possibly do that, Eva. What if you suddenly change your mind and escape after I accept his offer?"

"I won't escape… Okay, how about we sign a contract first? I don't mean the marriage contract. For now, maybe we can just sign a formal agreement of our bargain."

"Hmm… I guess that will do." He winked at her. Then, without delay, he took his phone from his pocket.

"All right, wait here, Eva. I'll go chat with Mr. Whitmore for a bit to keep him busy while our contract is being prepared. So, while I'm speaking with him, you better use this opportunity to think about this all over again." He leaned down and whispered in her ear, "Because once you sign, there will be no turning back."

CHAPTER 7

When Gage returned to the dining room, he was already holding a contract. It was all nicely printed out and bound in a clear folder.

"All right, I told Mr. Whitmore to wait for another hour," Gage said. He sat across from Eva. "Well? Still no change of mind?"

"No."

The corner of his lips lifted. "All right. Then why don't you take a look at this first?" He handed the papers over to her. "I am giving you a month to decide whether or not you will marry me. So, even if you have not accepted my main proposal yet, I will still accept Mr. Whitmore's offer and give you what you want. However, within that one month, I have my own conditions. It's all written out in there."

Eva nodded back at him, then immediately shifted her full attention to the papers in her hand. As she read on, she was pleased with what she had read from the contents so far. But she knew it was too early for her to celebrate.

And finally, she reached that most-awaited part.

[Condition #1: Party A must present to Party B one kiss every night.]

Eva lifted her gaze and peeked at him over the edge of the paper.

"One kiss… when you say one kiss…"

Gage nodded slowly as he kept his avid gaze on her. "I meant it as it sounds, Pet. Just one kiss… every night." He smiled at her devilishly. "It should not be that hard to do, right?"

Eva's mouth opened and closed a few times.

Speechless.

She finally choked out only after a few tries, "You're saying that you're not going to do more than just have that one kiss?"

He nodded, his eyes gleaming mischievously.

Eva could only take a deep breath and compose herself before dropping her head to continue reading.

[Consequence if condition #1 is not met: if Party A fails to present Party B with a kiss within one night, punishment will be meted out for Party A.]

Her brows knitted together.

[Punishment for failing to meet condition #1: Party B will be the one to initiate the kiss. Party B will be allowed to kiss Party A however long or in whatever way Party B wants. Party A has no right to deny Party B in this punishment.]

WHAT?!

Slowly, Eva peeked at him again. Somehow, the more she read through these conditions, the more she wanted to just… lose her temper. *What the hell is with these weird conditions?!*

Calm down, Eva, her inner demoness whispered to her, and she could only take a long deep breath, knowing that time was ticking and Mr. Whitmore was still waiting for them.

[Condition #1.1: Party A must not touch Party B while kissing Party B.]

[Consequence if condition #1.1 is not met: Party A must grant Party B one request. The request is fully up to Party B's discretion.]

Eva lifted her face, her eyes narrowing suspiciously.

Leisurely sitting there and leaning his chin against his knuckles, Gage simply stared back at her in an almost innocent manner. Eva wanted to blurt out something, but she bit her tongue and refrained once more.

She rested her temple on her fingers and continued reading, covering her face from his view with the paper.

[Condition #2: Party A will be Party B's bed warmer* every night.]

Eva suddenly choked.

Her eyes sharpened. Her fists clenched and unclenched a few times.

She knew that this man would definitely ask for something big in exchange, but she really didn't think he would ask for this.

Based on their previous conversation, she thought that he would not have such a thought of making her a...

Damn, did I just get tricked by this damned devil? He explicitly said that he was not keeping me to bed me, right? I was quite sure of what I heard earlier. Also, why the hell did he ask for one kiss and no touching if this was his bargain all along?!

She threw him a scornful look.

"Oh, don't jump to conclusions and get the wrong idea, Eva. There's a footnote there. Read it first." He pointed one long and elegant finger toward the bottom of the paper she was holding.

[Footnote: the term bed warmer is defined in literal terms.]

"W-what?"

"Yes, literally." Gage nodded. "You will be required to warm my bed, literally. Using your body, you go lie in my bed and warm it up until it is nice and toasty... every night, too."

Eva could only gape at him.

Why is there such a person as this?!

Now, now, just calm down, and let's keep reading until the end, her inner demoness whispered.

She could only obey.

[Consequence if Party A fails to carry out condition #2: Party A must permit Party B to do one intimate thing with Party A in bed. Party A is not allowed to reject Party B's request.]

A cough echoed out from Eva once again.

[Condition #2.2: Party A must not touch Party B while Party A is doing condition #2.]

[Consequence if Party A fails to do condition 2.2: Party A must grant one request from Party B.]

[Condition #3: Party A must live with Party B within the stipulated duration (30 days).]

[Condition #4: Party A must be home before dinner every night.]

[Condition #5: Party A must not get involved with another man within the stipulated duration (30 days).]

[Consequence if Party A fails to meet conditions #3, #4, and #5: Party B is free to choose a punishment for Party A, and Party A must accept one punishment.]

[Other important details: Party B must not do anything to Party A without Party A's permission. Party B must never impose any form of abuse on Party A. If Party A is not able to adhere to the consequences three times, Party B is allowed to revoke the contract, and Party A will be held liable. If Party B inflicts any kind of abuse(s), Party A is allowed to revoke the contract and will not be held liable.]

Eva was literally... completely... dumbstruck. She did not even know what to say or how to react after reading all that.

After moments of silence, she finally managed to speak.

"That's it? I mean, that is all, right?" Eva had to double-check and ask.

A wicked smile curved along Gage's lips. "You want more, Pet?"

"No! No... I mean, this—"

"Don't worry, Eva. As long as you meet the conditions, you won't even need to worry at all about the consequences. However, of course, it's still up to you to decide."

"So? What is your decision? Are you going to sign this agreement? Tick-tock, Pet... time's a running..." Gage gently tapped on his wristwatch. "You still have ten minutes. You can use the remaining time to think through it carefully. You still have the chance to back off, Eva. It's not too late."

Eva looked down and stared at the papers again.

Are you really going to do this? her inner demoness asked, and Eva's answer was a very firm yes.

But don't you think his conditions are way too suspicious? Let's be honest, it's almost ridiculous, you know?! Like, who the hell would ask for a literal bed warmer?

I know! But maybe he just needs a literal bed warmer because of some trauma or something like that. You know, some people really do have weird conditions, right? Maybe he is paranoid about using a heater in his room because he is afraid it might accidentally catch fire. Or maybe Mr. Acheron can only sleep in a bed that is warmed by someone else's body heat, and that's why he is asking for a literal bed warmer.

But what could have caused such a beautiful man to have this weird condition?

How would I know?! Extremely wealthy people are weird, anyway. And I, for one, don't have the damn luxury of time to think about that right now! I know this man is very suspicious, but this is my best and only choice right now. I told you. I will do anything to get my revenge!

And with that Eva decided to take the plunge.

There was no way that she was backing out of this! She knew that she could not find any offers that were better than this, no matter where she went, especially because of the rumors that had already tarnished her name.

If she did not go through with this, it would definitely take her a long time before she could stand up again, much less get the opportunity to exact her ultimate revenge.

This deal was the easiest, fastest, and most surefire way for her to achieve her goal.

It's alright, as long as… as long as Gage kept his word, there is nothing I would not pay to achieve my goal.

Slowly, Eva placed the paper on the table. Her lashes fluttered before she looked at him with an intent gaze.

Then she grabbed the ballpoint pen.

"You know that once you sign, there will be no turning back, right?" Gage said.

As she glanced up at him, her hands stopped mid-motion. She knew she was supposed to have a lawyer look at these agreements first, but no lawyer would probably allow her to sign these, and given her circumstances, she simply couldn't afford the luxury of being extra careful anymore.

"I am well aware of that, Mr. Acheron."

"You really are one brave woman." He leaned closer and whispered into her ear, "But keep this in mind, Eva. Once this contract between us is signed, you can't run anymore."

"I'm not going to run. As long as you keep your word that you will not abuse me, I can live with your demands and do my job properly."

"Good girl." He smiled at her, and with that, Eva signed the paper.

CHAPTER 8

Eva stared blankly at her signature.

There was no turning back now for her.

A sigh of relief escaped her lips before she handed him the pen that was still in her grasp.

Slowly, he took the pen from her. Then the corners of his lips lifted in an alluring curl before he, too, finally put down his own signature on the paper.

"All right, now that everything's settled," Gage said, breaking the silence after putting the signed papers back in the envelope with much satisfaction.

"Let's start with"—he reached out his hand and very quickly swiped the pair of glasses off the bridge of her nose—"getting rid of this," he added with a grin.

"Wait... what?!"

She frowned at him.

Confused.

What do my innocent glasses have to do with all of this?

He put her glasses back on her face, causing Eva to deepen her frown at him.

Gage stood languidly. "We're going out, Pet. Get ready."

"Mr. Acheron." Eva blocked his way and looked up at him with a stern face. "Since I am going to live with you from now on, I think it's time for you to stop calling me 'Pet.' I have a perfectly usable name. Please use it."

Gage cocked his head to the right, then flashed a slow and gorgeous smile at her. "Of course, if that's your wish..." he replied, then his voice seemed to turn into something so sinfully good as the next two words rolled off his lips. "Eva darling..."

Her cheeks burned hot, and a wicked half-smile graced his handsome face. It was as though her reaction to that little endearment had delighted him.

"You liked that," he purred.

"Absolutely not!" Eva's voice was loud as she quickly retorted, trying her hardest to regain her shattered composure. She refused to let this man keep playing around with her like this.

"Ah... What a shame! I really like that one better, too." He ran his fingers through his dark hair, and then he slipped away from her.

"Wait a moment, Mr. Acheron," she called out when she saw him heading toward the main door.

But he ignored her.

"Gage!"

He halted and looked over his shoulder. "Hmm?"

"I'm in my pajamas. You can't possibly want to take me out dressed like this, can you?"

His gaze traveled from the top of her head to the tips of her toes. He then gave an approving nod. "You look pretty good in those pink pajamas, though."

Eva glared at him heatedly. "I need to go to my house to get something to change into and pick up my personal things as well."

"I'll buy you everything you need…" He suddenly trailed off, then shrugged. "All right, I might as well allow you to go and say your goodbyes to your lovely house."

CHAPTER 9

Eva immediately started packing up while Gage leisurely looked around the living room of her apartment. She had asked him to wait at the parking garage, but the devil negotiated his way in with her.

His reason was that there might be paparazzi waiting to ambush her in front of her home and told her he was coming along solely for her protection.

Though skeptical, Eva could only relent, knowing he might be right.

"Do all of those things have sentimental value to you?" he asked, leaning his shoulder against the wall as he pointed his gaze at her luggage.

"These are my important things," she simply replied.

"I can buy you…" He paused, seemingly stopping himself from finishing that line.

"All right. It's fine with me even if you move everything over, too."

An accommodating smile lingered on his lips as he bent over and effortlessly carried two of her boxes.

Eva carried the rest of her baggage, and they finally left her house.

As they approached the elevator, she froze mid-step. Her eyes went wide with alarm as she abruptly grabbed Gage's arm.

"Reporters are here!" she breathed as she frantically pulled him back to the apartment.

Once they were inside, Eva closed the door behind them.

She took a moment to catch her breath.

"Gage. Listen," she held his gaze with an intense, serious stare. "I can't let them see me with you. I don't want your name to be dragged into the mud with mine when you just took on such an important position. My name has already been ruined, and it will stay ruined until I prove my innocence. I want you to go ahead without me. I'll wait here until they're gone. They can't be waiting here forever."

"You don't want anyone to see you…?"

"Correct." She clenched her jaw. "It's not a wise move if anyone will see me working with the Acherons. It could easily spark a destructive scandal in your company. And that is why I proposed working with you in the shadows. For now, I'll let them think I disappeared."

"Then later on, you will come at them out of the blue like a vengeful villain rising from the ashes?"

"That… doesn't sound so bad, does it?"

Gage leaned against the wall lazily, smiling. "Only making a noise when it's time to say checkmate, huh? Nice move."

Eva nodded. "I will play with them slow and dirty, the way they have played around with my life!" she hissed viciously. "I'll make them think I'm dead if need be. Let them lower their guard and be happy for a moment. It's more fun that way, don't you think? I will make sure to enjoy this game."

Gage smirked. "How evil… I like it!"

He put his hands inside his pocket and looked around the apartment again.

"I'm guessing this building is owned by your enemy, is that right? They actually let the reporters come all the way up here," he commented flippantly, and Eva nibbled the inside of her lips.

Anger was gleaming dangerously in her eyes once more as she clenched her fists into tight balls.

"Yes. This whole complex is owned by my ex-fiancé's parents," she replied coldly.

"I see. That makes a lot of sense, then."

"So please, we cannot go together. I will–"

"Can I see your closet?" he cut her off.

Eva creased her brows but eventually nodded. "Sure. It's over here."

Once they were inside, Gage scanned through her sets of clothes while Eva stood behind him with her arms crossed together.

"This is all you have?" Gage looked over his shoulder, and when Eva nodded, he rubbed the back of his neck. "Where are your dresses?"

"Over here."

Gage blinked at the rows of very formal and over-the-knee conservative dresses that she pointed at.

"You want me to disguise myself, right?" she asked, and before Gage could respond, she shoved him out of her dressing room. "Leave it to me."

CHAPTER 10

Leisurely sitting on the sofa with one of his long legs crossed over the other, Gage lifted his gaze.

He blinked at the sight of her.

"No one will recognize me now. Let's go," she said confidently.

She was now dressed in a loose black hoodie, a pair of baggy military print pants, black sunglasses, and a black face mask with a funny smiling teeth print.

Gage stood and approached her.

"I don't think so, Eva." He bent over and took her sunglasses off. "They'll be suspicious as soon as they see you, and I can already tell they will definitely mob you. You might be able to fool regular people. But these are experienced reporters who do this for a living."

"I know. They can take photos all they want, but it doesn't matter as long as they don't capture my face, right?"

"The reporters have surrounded and blocked the exit, remember? They will mob you on sight and might snatch that mask off or even pull your hoodie down. Don't underestimate what people can do."

Eva sighed. She knew that everything he said was indeed possible. And she never wanted to take any risk right now.

"Then I guess our only choice now is you will have to go out first. We can't be seen leaving together. I need to protect your name from all scandals at all costs. That is the least I can do."

"No. I won't leave you here."

"Please listen to—"

Gage pressed his finger against her lips. "Hush, Eva. Let me show you a better way out of this mess."

The doorbell echoed.

Before Eva could move to check who was ringing the doorbell, Gage had already walked past her and opened the door without even checking who was behind it first.

Eva almost yelled at him.

But she was too late. No, the damn devil was just too fast!

When a woman stepped through the door with a few shopping bags dangling over her arms, she sighed in relief.

Gosh, this devil is going to give me a heart attack!

The woman marched in confidently, smiling at Eva, and greeted her with a bright smile and a nod.

"This is Eloise. She's a good makeup artist," Gage immediately introduced the woman to her.

What? Makeup artist?

"She'll dress you up, Eva," Gage continued before he nodded at Eloise.

And with that, the two of them entered her dressing room again while Gage remained in the living room.

Eloise had her sit in front of the vanity table and then brought out a seemingly endless array of makeup from her bag.

Eva could only stare. Just how many things did she need?

"Alright, Miss Eva, are you ready?" Eloise asked.

She could only nod silently.

Eloise smiled.

"Don't be nervous, Miss. I will make sure that you love the outcome."

Without further ado, Eloise began her task.

Eva sat quietly, staring at herself in the mirror, expecting nothing. But as time passed, she couldn't help but glance at the artist in confusion.

"You're not planning to, like, change my appearance completely?" Eva commented. She had actually thought Eloise would perform that kind of makeup that alters someone's look entirely.

The artist paused and looked at her with surprise. "Of course not, miss. I will just... well, hide the imperfections and then enhance your natural beauty. You have really beautiful features, so it'll be an easy task."

Eva couldn't help but let out a self-mocking smile. "Oh please... you don't need to sugarcoat your words around me, Eloise. Don't worry, I won't be offended or anything."

Eloise blinked at her, silent for a few moments. "You really think you're not beautiful, don't you, miss?" she asked.

"Everyone thinks so too, I believe. And I can't blame them."

An awkward smile tugged at the corner of Eloise's lips before she sighed softly. "You are beautiful, Miss. Believe that. It's true that your bad skin needs some work and these puffy eyebags and dark circles need attention, but aside from these issues, your features are top-notch in my opinion. You have a small face and your big eyes... they're simply gorgeous. Your nose and lips are also perfect."

Eva lifted a brow, squinting her eyes as she tried to see herself clearly, even though she strongly believed that Eloise was exaggerating or lying for fear she might offend her. But sadly, without her glasses, all she could see was her own blurry face.

CHAPTER 11

Finally, Eloise emerged from behind the closed doors.

"The makeup's done, sir. She'll just need to put on the dress," she reported to Gage.

Gage gave her a slight nod.

"Okay, you may go. Thanks for the great job."

The woman politely bowed her head at her boss and immediately left the apartment.

Sitting on the sofa, Gage waited for Eva to come out. His long and elegant fingers languidly tapped on top of the couch.

But minutes ticked by, and Eva still did not come out.

Gage looked at his watch, and his brow lifted.

After waiting for a couple more minutes, he finally rose and knocked on the door.

"You are taking too long, Eva," he called out.

"Well, er... I don't think this dress is..."

Gage arched a brow again. But slowly, a small smile tugged at the corner of his lips.

"I'm opening the door," he warned before turning the door handle.

"Wait!" Eva called out, but she was too late.

The door was already open.

Still, Gage paused and waited for a moment. When she didn't say anything, he stepped inside.

The instant he saw her, he stilled in his steps.

Then a smile slowly crept onto his face.

CHAPTER 12

Eva turned away to hide her face from him.

"I'll get changed," she said.

"No, Eva." He moved closer, stopping right behind her. "You want to hide, don't you?" he asked, and she couldn't help but notice how the temperature seemed to skyrocket just because he was so near.

"Take a look at yourself, Eva," he added.

She glanced at herself in the mirror again and swallowed thickly.

The woman staring back at her looked... so different. She was sophisticated, alluring, beautiful, and... sexy. Not at all like the Eva she knew. She could no longer see the proper and strictly formal businesswoman.

Her face, her hairstyle, her black mini dress clinging tightly to her body, and her legs—legs that now seemed impossibly long—evoked a strange, unfamiliar feeling in her. It was truly insane, and it may not make any sense, but the ugly Eva was indeed nowhere to be seen!

"This is how you hide in plain sight, Pet," he continued.

When she shifted her gaze toward his reflection, their eyes met. The sight of him standing there behind her, so tall and imposing, with a gaze that seemed to hold pride, slowly ebbed the strange feeling within her.

She wasn't entirely sure if that was pride she saw in his eyes, but regardless, it helped calm her nerves.

"Of course, this will only work because nobody has seen you like this before." He smiled at her through the mirror and then carefully placed an elegant pair of black sunglasses on her face.

And with that, her all-new look was complete.

He was right.

Even she could barely recognize herself in this outfit and makeover! She had never worn her hair down in public. Only in her own room did she take off her tight hair ties and thick, old-fashioned glasses.

"Hold on to my arm," Gage said as they finally stepped out of her apartment. She complied obediently but paused at the threshold.

"Wait… but my baggage—"

"Don't worry about them, Eva. I already asked someone to deal with everything. I assure you your things will be taken care of. If even one single thing is missing, or someone dares breach your privacy by peeking at your belongings, you can hold me accountable. I'll gouge their eyes out myself."

79

She could only blink at him. He was smiling like the mischievous devil he was as he said that last line, but why did she feel like he would actually do it if someone dared mess with her things?

Nah… stop overthinking.

"Fine. I'll trust you with this then, Mr. Acheron," she said.

"Good. Ready?"

"Yes."

Gage led her out, whispering, "Just relax and don't be stiff."

This was making her a little nervous, but at the same time, an unfamiliar thrill zinged through her body.

"Just walk confidently. Head up, chest forward. Treat the reporters like they're irrelevant bystanders, or better yet, insignificant ants by the roadside." He winked at her with relaxed mischief, and Eva couldn't help but flash him a wicked smile.

"Let them come! I'm not scared of them," she declared.

"Good girl."

"Though I'm a little worried I might trip. I don't usually wear this kind of high heels…"

"Don't worry. I'm right here. I won't let you trip."

As they walked down the quiet corridor, Gage inched closer to Eva. Her shoulder pressed against his, and she tightened her grip around his forearm. The strong and firm muscles she clung to provided her with an unexpected sense of security. She couldn't believe how secure she felt in that moment… as if he would always protect her, no matter what.

To her, this felt unreal. Strange.

She was the type of person who was always wary of everyone. Even with people she had known for a long time, she never dared to give her complete trust, no matter how nice or capable they seemed. It was something taught to her—that the only people she should fully trust were her family.

That teaching felt funny to her now, but she knew that not trusting just anyone was definitely a wise move.

And yet, here she was, actually feeling all this towards a man she had just met.

The feel of his hand taking hers off his arm snapped her out of her thoughts. Just as she was about to turn to him, he entwined their fingers. The sensation of his large palm against her smaller one nearly made her stumble.

And the warmth of his hand was just a bit too distracting!

As they got closer to where the reporters were gathered, Eva lifted her chin. Somehow, she wasn't worried about being recognized. Her confidence was growing, and she could only attribute it to the imposing man walking next to her.

No matter how he acted around her, Eva knew that Gage exuded an uncommon aura. He was the type of person who could effortlessly make a crowd part without saying a single word. And it was proven when the reporters saw them coming and opened up a path, as if it was the most natural thing to do.

None of them lifted their cameras. They simply stared as though in a daze. No one made a single move aside from their heads, following them until they reached the elevator doors.

Everyone was quiet. The only sound was the soft click of their heels against the carpeted floor.

The elevator doors opened.

Gage's hand moved to the small of Eva's back, then curled around and settled naturally on her waist. They both stepped inside.

When the elevator doors finally closed, Eva let out a long, deep breath.

"See? The easiest way to hide is not to hide at all," Gage said with a proud smile.

Eva could not help but smile back. She had enjoyed the thrill. She could hardly believe that none of those reporters actually moved at all. It was almost as if someone had hypnotized them!

As their car drove out of the building complex, Gage began to talk about his plans. "I will be taking over in three days. So, you have three days to perfect your disguise, Eva."

Eva looked at him with a questioning gaze.

"From now on, you'll be Evelyn Lee, my smart, alluring, and sexy personal secretary and assistant," he explained, glancing at her with a serious look.

"All right," Eva replied without a tinge of hesitation. She didn't need any more explanation about why they had to walk down this road. And now that she had experienced herself that disguising actually worked, her confidence in going through this plan skyrocketed.

And becoming his secretary was also the perfect position for her to do all his work for him, as she had promised. She needed to be stuck with him at all times, if possible. That way, she would also be able to watch him closely. And it was not only to make sure he would not do anything scandalous to ruin his name but also to prevent anything that might cause his own downfall. She knew his face and body were definitely trouble magnets!

"Good." He nodded with approval. "We will discuss this more when I get back."

When their car passed by XY Corporation's building, Eva kept her eyes glued on it. Her eyes hardened, and viciousness flashed deep within them.

"You're not actually scheming up a plan on how to burn the whole building down, are you?" Gage asked, humor gleaming in his eyes as he glanced at her.

"Yes, I want to burn them all to hell," she uttered absentmindedly.

Gage smiled at her response.

"You sound like a villain right now, Miss Lee."

"It's their fault. They have painted me as one. So, I should not disappoint my dear so-called family members and make sure I turn out as they view me."

"How scary," Gage commented lightly as the corners of his lips curled up.

Eva finally looked at him and saw the corner of his lips still lifted as his gaze was focused on the road.

Her inner demoness came out. *Why does he look like he is excited about something? Look at that gorgeous smile.*

Eva shook her head. *Stop it! He's just probably excited to watch some drama in action.*

But again, her inner demoness scoffed. *You're not serious, are you? Do you really think this hot devil is smiling like that because he's a fan of drama?*

Who knows? I just don't want to think about him right now. He's impossible to figure out anyway. Eva silently groaned, then her fists clenched as she glanced at XY's building again through the side mirror.

CHAPTER 13

"I will be gone for three days," Gage informed her as soon as he parked his car in front of his mansion.

"Three days?" Eva whipped around and looked at him with slightly creased brows. "Where are you going?"

"New York."

With the city-state of Letran located just south of Canada and north of the US on the East Coast, New York was the closest major city. He should be able to make the trip in just a few hours. But three days... wasn't that a bit too long?

"What are you going to do there?" she asked straightforwardly. "Since you said you're lazy, business shouldn't be your purpose for going, I believe?"

"Well... I'm heading there for something else."

Eva narrowed her eyes.

"What exactly is this 'something else,' Mr. Acheron?"

He lifted a brow, his eyes gleaming with mischief again. "I'm a healthy bachelor, Eva. And I only have three days left before I get stuck with this new job I've thrown myself into. So, I might as well go fool around while I can. Right?"

"You can't," she blurted out seriously, belatedly realizing she might actually end up irritating him with how strict she sounded.

But to her surprise, her response seemed to amuse him rather than irritate him.

He flashed a slow smile before leaning his elbow against the wheel and resting his temple against his knuckles. Then he trained his smoldering gaze on her without saying anything for a short moment, causing Eva to wonder if her blurting out things might have indeed started things off on the wrong foot.

"You're acting like my wife already," he said sexily, as if he truly adored the very idea he just spouted.

That made Eva blush a little.

But before she could respond, Gage continued. "Too bad you didn't accept my proposal yet. Don't you know that I am the kind of guy who listens to his wife's orders?" he said with a slight smile on his somewhat serious-looking face.

Eva did not know if he was just teasing her or if he was actually serious about his statement!

"N-no. Well... I mean... you mentioned in the contract that I needed to give you a kiss every night and warm your bed. If you leave, how will I be able to carry these requirements out then?"

"This one's on me, so it won't be counted toward the agreed-upon contract. And you didn't say anything about this matter when we signed, Pet," he replied, staring at her with full interest. Then his grin became even more playful. "You should've also counter-suggested some consequences for me if I fail to be present by your side every night."

Eva could not help but throw him a sharp glance at his comment.

Why is he suggesting this now? And did he forget that the contract was already finalized when he showed it to me?

She could only inhale a sharp breath. There was no use talking about that now, anyway. The contract was already signed.

However, she could not just let him go running off like this.

She understood that she was not in any position to stop him since she was not his girlfriend or fiancée, but... what if... what if he was caught in a scandal and that would then ruin his name? That was the last thing she wanted to happen!

Her plans for revenge had barely started! She could not have anything mess it up! Not even the person who would be the one providing her the opportunity to exact her vengeance.

"If I become your girlfriend now, will you still go and fool around with other women?" she asked. Straightforward. Serious.

Her question made Gage subtly raise his brow.

"You think I'm the type of man who will get it on with other girls while I have a girlfriend?"

"Well… men nowadays love to do that, don't they? They're never satisfied with just one woman. And it is a well-known thing that the more loaded a man is, the more ladies he has by his side. And you, Mr. Acheron, are the definition of loaded."

Eva had met too many men who seemed to view cheating as a normal part of their lives. Even her ex-fiancé… *That bastard! He must have been cheating on me since we were in college!*

Suddenly, he reached out and pinched her cheek gently, causing Eva to snap out of her thoughts and look at him with confusion.

"Worry not, Eva. I'll come back to you without any scandals. That I can promise you." He flashed her a small but reassuring smile.

Eva blinked at him. *How did he know I was worried about that? It's like he can read me like a book!*

She stared hard at him as if trying to scrutinize his every expression. But eventually, she gave in and said with her signature no-nonsense tone, "If you don't keep your promise, I will hold you accountable." And as an additional, unspoken warning, she trained a laser-beam-like gaze on him.

His smile widened, and he looked amused again. "Of course."

"I'm very serious here."

"I know. Also, just for your information, I don't do girlfriend proposals, Eva. I'm only interested in marriage proposals."

Eva blinked. Speechless for the nth time!

"So, if you want to ground me, just do one simple thing." He let go of her cheek and rubbed the skin he gently pinched with the pad of his thumb, even though he did not hurt her at all. "Marry me, and I'm all yours."

When her mouth dropped open, a sexy chuckle echoed inside the car. "But there is no rush, Eva. You have a month to think about it. So, take your time and think through it carefully."

His smile faded, and his tantalizing eyes seemed to suddenly turn smoldering hot. He leaned back, but his face was still tilted toward her.

"Now, since I'm still here and it is already night, how about you keep your end of the bargain? You must give me my kiss before I go."

Eva fell silent at his words, and when her gaze wandered and landed at his mouth, she felt her pulse quicken.

"Nervous?" A teasing yet wolfish grin flashed across his features.

Her gaze at him sharpened. "It's natural for any first timer to feel nervous, Mr. Acheron."

A brief silence.

Then a slow frown crossed Gage's face before it was quickly replaced by surprise.

"Wait… are you saying that you've never been kissed before?"

"I'm saying I have never kissed someone before where I'm the one who needs to initiate and do the kissing."

"Oh."

Gage leaned back.

She did not quite see the look on his face when he heard her explanation as he had turned away, put his hand over his mouth, and cleared his throat. "I see…"

When he moved his hand away from his face, his wolfish grin returned. He leaned in, tucking a loose wave of her hair behind her ear.

His fingers lingered as he spoke. "Don't worry, Pet. Just relax. I'm totally fine even if you want to carry out a few trials to get yourself familiarized with the process. I'm giving you the freedom to practice on me right now."

That made her blush again.

Why is his voice suddenly sounding so tempting?

"I don't need practice, Mr. Acheron." She managed to keep her face straight as she answered him smoothly.

Then, without warning, Eva twisted her body to face him fully. One hand braced herself on his seat while the other moved to lightly cup his face.

But before she could touch him, her hand halted midway, remembering his damn condition that she couldn't touch him while kissing him and that she would be punished if she did.

So, she grabbed onto his collar instead.

Gage smiled. "Bold gi—"

Eva's lips unceremoniously crashed against his.

He froze.

Then she pulled away.

"Done," she said.

As their gazes held, Gage bit down on his lower lip. He looked so speechless.

When Eva slowly retreated back to her seat, a breath that almost sounded like a laugh escaped Gage's lips.

Eva glanced at him, her voice flat, brows arched, though her ears were still a bit red. "What? You didn't specify what kind of kiss, remember?"

An amused chuckle erupted. "Well, true. You are right again."

He ran his fingers through his hair before climbing out of the car, still smiling as if he couldn't get over how their first kiss had ended faster than a second.

Eva moved to open the door as she saw him walk around to her side, but he beat her to it.

Stepping out, she found herself trapped between Gage's tall frame and the car.

"That was one memorable kiss, I must say," he muttered softly, looking as though that kiss was still amusing him to no end.

But a moment passed, and his expression changed. His gaze seemed to darken as he leaned over her, the playful air vanishing.

It was already twilight.

And somehow… Gage in the dim light felt… different.

Eva suddenly realized that without bright lights and those playful smirks plastered on his face, Gage seemed to look and feel completely different from the lazy and rich heir persona that he usually displayed.

A completely mysterious air clung to him now, and for a moment, she felt as though there was something off about him… something that made the tiny hairs along her spine stand on end.

His eyes, which looked dark during the day, now seemed to have lightened, as if someone had replaced his black pupils with hazel ones. She had heard of people whose eye colors changed, but was this really possible? How could his eyes brighten in the dark? Or was it just the lighting?

"I've arranged everything. Just focus on what you need to prepare," he said, pulling her from her observations.

"I got it," Eva responded sharply.

"Well then." He paused, his gaze sweeping across her face and lingering on her lips a moment too long before returning to her eyes.

He leaned closer, whispering near her ear, "See you in three days, Eva."

And with that, he walked back to the driver's side and slid smoothly into his car.

As she watched his car drive off and vanish from sight, Eva absentmindedly reached over and touched her lips, remembering how soft and warm his lips were against hers when she had crashed her lips on his.

She shook her head. Shifting her focus, she turned to face the mansion before her.

When they had left earlier, she discovered that the luxurious mansion was actually located in the famous Soleil Heights.

This upscale residential area known for its stunning views of the city and the ocean was probably the most exclusive place in the entirety of Letran. Even the Youngs couldn't acquire a property in Soleil Heights because, as she had learned, the Acherons, the owners of the entire area, weren't selling a single piece of land.

As she stood there, Eva couldn't help but marvel at the grand château-like residence, which she now believed was built in the early 1800s.

Her eyes traced the tall arched windows, the ornate wrought-iron railings, the detailed dormer windows, and the multiple towers and turrets that were topped with conical roofs.

The mansion was surrounded by expansive landscaped gardens, including manicured lawns and ornate fountains.

The entire estate truly screamed luxury, and Eva could only think of how much was the exact cost in maintaining such a place.

She also wondered if this mansion had been the Acheron family's residence for generations. As far as she knew, the main Acheron residence, where George Acheron lived, was not located in Soleil Heights.

"Miss Eva?" a voice called.

Turning, Eva faced an older man in his fifties, flanked by two maids.

The trio immediately introduced themselves before they then led her into the mansion.

They revealed they had been the caretakers of the house for many years—the man as the butler and the two maids responsible for maintaining the home's cleanliness.

And when Eva inquired about the maid Gage mentioned who had run away, none of them could provide her an answer.

Before Eva knew it, three days had quickly gone by.

It was currently an hour to midnight, but Gage had yet to come back home. Eva sat in his favorite chair—she assumed it was his favorite—by the fireplace with a laptop on her knees.

The past three days had been peaceful yet busy for her.

She had diligently followed his instructions, completing all the tasks she needed to do.

The only thing that bothered her was Gage himself. The man hadn't even had the decency to call or send a message, leaving her feeling as if he had vanished into thin air. She had occasionally inquired with the butler and maids about his well-being, but they only reassured her that their master would certainly return.

What frustrated her most was that she didn't have his number saved. So she told herself that if he did not return home that night, she would call Mr. Whitmore to inquire about his whereabouts. Then she would find that elusive devil and drag him back herself if necessary.

CHAPTER 14

The elegant clock ticked on.

Its faint sound echoed gently in the silence of the vast living room.

Just a second before the hour hand struck midnight, a lightning strike struck. Its light was like a sudden blast that illuminated the mansion in the blink of an eye.

The thunder roared next, and when its sound faded, a heavy silence reigned.

The curtains moved ever so slightly.

Then he entered.

Gage.

He was dressed in all black. His midnight hair was tousled and damp as though he had walked through a windy squall.

A menacing aura clung to him as he moved like a shadow. Graceful. Quiet.

The moment he stepped into the slightly bright area of the vast living room, his face was finally unveiled.

His expression was blank. Emotionless. Dangerous as hell yet still as tempting as sin.

His silent footstep halted.

And the moment his gaze landed on the chair by the fireplace and found Eva sleeping there, the darkness that seemed to erase the emotions in his eyes were gone.

The corner of his lips lifted before he glided closer to her sleeping form.

When he reached her, he bent over.

His gaze shifted from the laptop on her lap to her hand, which had fallen to her side and then back to her serene, sleeping face.

She looked at peace and vulnerable.

She was wearing the tiger pajamas he had told the maids to place in her wardrobe. And just as he had imagined, they looked incredibly cute on her.

"Adorable…" he whispered.

The usually fierce little tigress now looked like an extremely adorable, fluffy kitten.

His smile spread wider across his handsome face, and just like that, his aura completely shifted. The danger was completely gone. The dark, heavy air around him disappeared.

Lifting his hand, he reached out to touch her cheek when suddenly, he paused just before his fingertips brushed against her skin. His gaze stared at his hand, and the sight of a dark red stain on his fingertips made him clench his fist instead.

Slowly, he stood. He stared at her a little longer before he turned and left the living room in silence.

Gage headed directly to the bathroom and started undressing.

He stepped into the shower. There was no visible wound on his skin, but the water cascading down his perfect body turned into a reddish-pink as it hit the marble floor.

CHAPTER 15

The very first sight that greeted Eva the moment she opened her eyes was a man's face.

"What a glorious face…" she murmured.

Just as she lifted her hand to touch his skin, her sleepy eyes widened. "Wait… Gage!? You're back!"

"Good morning, darling," he greeted, smiling at her. And his morning voice… damn… She felt like she had just been introduced to what an angel of the dark's voice sounded like.

She sprung up in an instant.

"We're not already late, are we?" she exclaimed and then glanced at the clock and gasped. "Oh my God! We're going to be late!"

She jumped from the bed as if the house was on fire.

"Relax, Eva. I am the owner. And yeah, the boss is not strict at all, so you don't have to be—"

"Get up and get ready!" she cut him off.

But Gage just smiled and lazily threw his head back on the pillow, shutting his eyes.

"Eva, it's fine even if we're a couple of hours late. We're the bosses, they—"

Suddenly, Eva seized his collar. She loomed over him, glaring.

"No. I can never let us be late for the first day of work. Never on my watch! So please get your ass off this bed now or else…"

He opened his eyes.

"Or else?" He lifted a brow, his gaze now gleaming with mischief. "What are you going to do, my little tiger?"

Eva bit her lip in frustration. She could not believe that this man was trying her patience as soon as he came back! *He did say that he was lazy, but… oh God… is he really like this?!*

She was not sure if she would survive if this became a daily occurrence! She was used taking care only of herself for years since she studied abroad. Having to deal with a man like this as soon as she woke up was certainly something entirely new to her!

"Do you know how the prince awakened Sleeping Beauty? I think that method would definitely work on me, too, Pet. Why don't we give it a try?" he drawled.

Eva's jaw dropped. *My God! What the hell's wrong with this creature?!*

When he shut his eyes again, she drew in a long breath through clenched teeth.

Glancing at the clock once more, Eva bit her lip.

She no longer had time to argue! So she bent down and unceremoniously pressed her lips to his. The kiss was brief, lasting less than a fleeting second.

Pulling away immediately, she hissed at him, "Now get up, damn it! Don't you dare keep trying my patience, Mr. Acheron. Or I swear I will make you regret it!"

He chuckled, letting her pull him up to a sitting position. "Another punch in the lips, hm, darling?" he commented teasingly, amused, but now letting her drag him off the bed. "I would like to dare and try your patience again next time to see what you'll do—"

"Just stop fooling around and get ready," Eva barked. "If we are late, I swear!"

CHAPTER 16

"Where is Mr. Acheron?" Eva asked Eloise as they descended the stairs.

For the past three days, Eloise had been closely assisting her and taking her to salons.

It was truly amazing to see how much her skin improved in such a short time! However, of course, she still believed that nothing compared to the remarkable transformation Eloise's makeup skills had achieved on her face.

Eloise truly understood her assignment that she had to make her look different from the original prim and proper Eva Young that people knew her to be. Her looks needed to be turned from a Plain Jane into a femme fatale. Because she was now Evelyn Lee, Gage Acheron's sophisticated and hot personal secretary.

She was not planning to depend on Eloise forever, though. She might be ignorant of the ins and outs of makeup and fashion, but she had already started observing everything Eloise was doing so that one day she could do all of these things by herself.

Well… hopefully.

"He's already dressed and prepped, Miss Lee. He's currently waiting outside for you," Eloise answered.

Eva sighed in relief.

She was a little worried that the man was going to act difficult again and frustrate her with all his antics.

Once she stepped out of the main door, the first thing she saw was him leaning against the car.

He was tastefully dressed in a tailored black suit, well suited for his tall and broad frame, and was now looking as handsome as the devil. He was always handsome, but seeing Gage in a suit was just…

It was as if black suits were invented just for him to wear.

The combination of his impeccably tailored suit, dark hair, and piercing eyes almost gave him the aura of a sophisticated Mafia don. It was as if this guy had stepped straight out of a high-end magazine photoshoot, exuding an effortless, intoxicating charm that was just impossible to ignore.

This man… Does he have to look so distractingly perfect all the time?

When their eyes met, the corner of his lips curled up.

"Hey, you look amazing," he remarked.

"Thank you, sir," Eva simply replied.

103

Eloise had told her that Gage was the one who chose her outfit today. A tight black high-waisted skirt and a red V-necked shirt paired with a pair of black pointy heels.

She was amazed at how she looked when she had stared at herself in the mirror earlier. The outfit, makeup, and contact lenses she wore truly worked their magic, transforming her into a different person.

Eloise had told her that a significant change in hairstyle, clothing, and makeup done by an exceptionally skilled makeup artist could dramatically alter someone's overall appearance. And she was absolutely right.

Eva felt confident that no one would recognize her because even she almost couldn't. It might sound exaggerated, but she realized it was partly because she had never truly stared at her own face. She only looked in the mirror to ensure her face was clean or when she needed to hype or encourage herself. But during those moments, she couldn't recall if she was actually looking at her own face. It always felt like she was just staring at her own blue eyes.

Moreover, she had worn glasses her entire life and had never really seen herself without them, which was certainly one of the biggest factors as well.

She believed that everyone who used to know her, including her so-called family and ex-fiancé, would definitely not recognize her. Reflecting on it, she realized that they barely ever looked at her when she was with them. She had never paid much attention to it and thought it was normal. They had been like that since she was young. Even during conversations, there were only occasional glances. Many times, her so-called mother and father didn't even bother lifting their heads to look at her and simply spoke.

Her throat tightened at these thoughts and realizations.

There had been so many signs, too many signs, that she had meant nothing to them all this time.

As the car sped on, Eva took a long, quiet breath. She needed to stop thinking about them now. She needed her mind focused on nothing but this very important first day of work.

Focus, Eva.

But just as she started shifting her entire attention to more important thoughts, she felt something unusual. She tried to ignore it, but as minutes passed, it continued. So she turned and looked in Gage's direction.

He was staring at her.

She had never caught anyone looking at her for more than a few moments, much less staring at her face this way. Well, Julian did, back when they were younger.

But she thought now that it must have been because her face and skin were still young and clear then. Because for a long time—maybe since she started officially working at the company about six years ago—she realized she couldn't remember his gaze lingering on her, much less staring at her.

Now, now, I thought you were going to stop thinking about them, her inner demoness sighed.

Trying her best to refocus and clear her mind, Eva glanced at her wristwatch and then spoke to the chauffeur. "Please speed up. We need to be there on time."

"Easy, Miss Lee. There is no need to rush. Just sit there and relax. We'll get there when we get there," Gage said calmly.

He was incredibly relaxed, as if he were not on his way for the first day of work as the new CEO of a huge company but on his way to a chill vacation.

Eva breathed out slowly, controlling herself from losing her composure once again. She forced herself to sit back and shut her mouth because he was right. She needed to just stay calm and composed.

Usually, staying calm and collected at times like this was never a problem for her. But this was different because she had to put on an act and watch herself closely to ensure she wouldn't mess up her disguise.

"Eva, darling?" he broke the silence, causing Eva to shoot him a stern look.

"Stop calling me that, Mr. Acheron. We're technically at work right now, so please address me accordingly."

"You know… for a moment there, you looked very much like Evangeline Young when you glared and spoke so strictly like that. Evelyn Lee should be a sweet and sophisticated lady, don't you think?" he commented lightly as his eyes returned a challenging but still soft look back at her.

A long and deep sigh was drawn from her lips.

Suddenly, she remembered the thing that she had been pondering over while Eloise was doing her makeup earlier.

"By the way, Mr. Acheron," she started, her expression back to being calm. "Why did you sleep in my bed last night? Our contract stated that I only needed to warm your bed. You can't claim it was because I didn't warm your bed." Eva fixed him with a probing gaze. "Last night was an exception since you didn't return home on time. According to our agreement, if the fault lies with you, I shouldn't be blamed. So your decision to enter my bedroom and even sleep on my bed for whatever reason, without my permission, is something we need to address immediately."

Gage remained silent, seemingly observing her.

Then he gently bit his lower lip, releasing it slowly in a manner that could only be described as alluring, before allowing a charming smile to spread across his face.

"Of course, we can discuss it if that's what you wish," he replied as he positioned himself and faced her fully.

"So, explain to me, Mr. Acheron. You jumped into my bed solely because your own bed was ice-cold and not for a more dubious or malicious reason, correct?" Eva asked, her eyes narrowing. *You better confirm that's the reason, you... big wolf!*

He bit his lip again, and she was certain it was to prevent a grin from spreading across his face.

"Malicious reasons..." he echoed. "Would you care to elaborate on that? Maybe you could provide some specific examples? I seem to find myself at a loss to understand your meaning."

Eva closed her eyes, taking another deep, calming breath to steady herself. "You're avoiding the issue again, Mr. Acheron. Let's address it directly without beating around the bush, shall we?"

"Relax, Eva. This isn't a business discussion."

"Yes. But to me, this is as serious as any business talk."

"All right." He nodded. "You're right. The reason is my bed was cold, and…"

"And?" she prompted, wanting to get to the bottom of it.

"Do you really want to know the true reason? It might be better if—"

"Mr. Acheron," she interjected sharply, using her usual authoritative professional tone. "We need to finish this discussion before we arrive at our destination. So, please just say it."

"Fine. Since you insist so strongly, Miss Lee," he conceded with a tone that suggested surrender, yet his expression remained casual, almost nonchalant. Eva found herself fighting the urge to pinch his somewhat arrogant yet undeniably handsome face.

"It's because you didn't let me go."

Eva blinked. "W-what?"

Of all the things she expected him to say, this was not it!

Gage elegantly shrugged.

"You fell asleep on the chair last night. So I had decided to be the ever so gallant Prince Charming and carried you to your room. Just as I was tucking you into your bed and wanted to leave, you suddenly grabbed on to me and didn't want to let go. You were hugging me and clutching hard on my shirt. And since it was already very late, I didn't want to disturb you or wake you up. So I allowed you to just chain me to you." He recounted the events with a neutral and matter-of-fact tone, as if he were delivering a business report, his expression devoid of any hint of mischief throughout.

Eva wanted to believe he was fabricating the story, but the usual playful spark that lit his eyes whenever he teased her was not there. In fact, his gaze looked downright serious and truthful.

Blushing slightly in embarrassment, Eva cleared her throat and looked away. "That can't be, Mr. Acheron. Why would I cling to you?"

He let out a sexy chuckle. "You looked really cute last night, Eva," he said. "Like an adorable little kitten. I really decided to stay docile and quiet because I knew that if I were to wake that little kitten up, she would then turn into a fierce tiger and"—he threw her a heart-stopping look— "I might get eaten alive."

For a moment, Eva felt dumbfounded. And before she could open her mouth to speak, the driver spoke.

"We're here, sir, ma'am," the chauffeur reported, and Eva finally realized the car had already stopped.

Oh damn! How can I just forget everything when this man is...

A soft groan escaped her, but she quickly regained her composure. This was not the moment to continue their conversation, because it was now showtime!

"Are you ready?" she asked him, only to see him being super relaxed, as if nothing amazing or interesting was going to happen. *This man...*

She remembered how nerve-racking it was for her that very first day she had taken over XY, and here he was...

Closing her eyes, Eva took another deep breath. Upon reopening them, her demeanor transformed—soft yet composed, with a delicate smile gracefully adorning her face. "Shall we go, sir?" she said, now fully personifying the poised and impeccable Evelyn Lee.

Gage stilled for a moment but eventually nodded with pleasure. "That expression really looks good on you, Miss Lee."

"Thank you, sir," she politely replied before stepping out of the car first.

There were already lines of employees waiting outside the entrance, ready to welcome their new CEO to work.

As Eva stood there waiting for her boss, she did her best to maintain her composure, telling herself that there must not be the slightest mistake or crack in her new persona. It should come to her as naturally as breathing and blinking. Having practiced this repeatedly over the last three days, she was quite confident in her ability to maintain the façade.

It shouldn't be too difficult, as it was only necessary while they were outside his office. Once out of view, there was no longer a need to feign a delicate, alluring, and friendly smile for appearances.

Gage glanced over at her before taking the lead. She smoothly fell into step right behind him, not missing a beat as they passed the rows of employees. Eva noticed their shocked expressions—the kind reserved for sighting something so beautifully unreal.

Well, it did not surprise her at all. Because this man before her could probably turn the heads of even the straightest men to the point that they would want him dead for being too damned handsome for his own good!

Soon, they encountered the famous and well-respected chairman of ACEON at the entrance to the meeting room.

Mr. George Acheron, the renowned head of the Acheron family, still looked quite good-looking even at his age. He was definitely the kind women would love to call sugar-daddy, not only because of his money and single status, but also because he was certainly one of those whom people described as someone who aged like fine wine.

"I can't believe my lazy grandson is finally emerging from his den," George said as he scrutinized his grandson from head to toe.

"I also can't believe it, Grandfather," Gage replied. "Normally... I should still be having my beauty sleep right about now."

"It makes me wonder who managed to whoop your ass to get up and go to work."

"A certain tigress," Gage muttered softly in amusement. "She didn't whoop my ass, though. She only punched my lips."

"That's one brazen tigress! She is certainly someone you deserve." George looked a little closer at Eva and smiled. "So, it's her, huh…?"

Gage signaled at Eva, and she stepped closer to them.

"This is Evelyn Lee," Gage introduced. "My personal secretary. Miss Lee, my grandfather."

"It's a pleasure to meet you, Mr. Acheron." Eva gave the elder her most beautiful smile as she accepted his handshake.

George leaned in a little closer to her. "You are the lady he's currently hiding in his house, right?"

The question flustered Eva for a moment, and she could not respond to him immediately. "Um—"

"You and I must meet up and have tea sometime, Ms. Lee." George leaned away and smiled at Eva once again before he turned and entered the meeting room.

CHAPTER 17

After the meeting, the tour in the building and other formalities for the takeover, their busy first day finally concluded.

However, for the little fierce tigress, the day was far from over.

The CEO's office was quiet and still.

Gage was lazing on the couch, browsing on his tablet while Eva sat busily typing away in the CEO's chair. Their arrangement had been like that for hours now.

His gaze lifted to the wall clock and watched the seconds hand move. The moment it hit 11:00, he stood up from the couch.

Hands tucked in his pockets, he walked over to the busy woman, who remained intensely focused on her work. She looked like the world might crash and burn but she would still focus solely on what she was doing.

He had refrained from teasing her since they entered the building this morning because he could see she was trying her very best. And all day long, she was, as expected, simply exceptional. She not only managed to keep that soft smile on her face, but her temperament and poise were also impeccable.

He was honestly awed and proud especially since he experienced himself how easily she could snap and give him that if-looks-could-kill signature gaze of hers.

And now here she was, sitting there like work was her lifeline and that right now she was in a quiet battle. The way she looked... her expression, her eyes, the set of her lips, and her insane focus... damn, he could watch her all day, all night.

A smile spread across his lips as he sat on the edge of the mahogany desk, his gaze never leaving her.

Still, Eva ignored him. As if she did not notice him at all. He had actually been gloriously ignored since the moment she had sat her tooshie down on that chair and no one was around but them.

But his smile only widened. Not that he was happy at the way she was ignoring him. He was simply amused and amazed. This silence wasn't bad. Her presence alone was enough for him. And this sight of her... just being the fierce and intense female warrior that she was... without being distracted to anything or anyone around her... it was simply a sight to behold.

But it was time for a break. It was time for him to intervene since this fierce lady seemed to have forgotten not just him, her handsome partner, but also time itself.

Silently, he walked to a door, and when he came out, a bottle of wine and two wine glasses were in his hands.

Without saying a word, he popped open the bottle and poured it into the glasses.

The smell of the full-bodied wine finally pulled Eva's attention from the laptop. Oh damn… did the wine just beat him?

When she finally looked up at him, he offered her a glass.

Pulling away from the table, she accepted the glass of wine.

The soft smile she gave him was… damn alluring.

Lifting her glass at him, she uttered, "Cheers to you, sir. Congratulations on being inaugurated as the new CEO."

"Thank you, Miss Lee. Cheers."

They both sipped on their glass and after that, he raised his glass again. "And cheers to you, too. This marks the beginning of your new journey, Eva."

Eyes gleaming, her smile slowly widened into a grin. "Thank you," she said. Then her gaze turned fierce. "Yes. This marks the beginning of my journey to vengeance."

And once again, their glasses clinked together.

CHAPTER 18

"I guess... I'm going to be the one handling the investigations on your case," Gage said, casually shifting his stance and sliding a hand into his pocket.

"My case?" Eva frowned a little as she eyed him over the rim of her wine glass.

"Eva Young's fraudulent behavior and misconduct in her workplace."

Eva blinked. Then, slowly, she put her wine glass down. The soft sound of the glass clinking against the desk seemed overly loud because of the sudden thick silence that blanketed the atmosphere.

"You... you will investigate my case? Why?" she asked, genuinely surprised and a little confused. She had never expected him to voluntarily offer her his help on this matter.

He shrugged, twirling his glass before he slightly tilted his head.

"Why? Hmm... because I'm bored?"

"Please answer me seriously, sir." She directed him a sharp look.

"I'm serious, Eva. And this matter interests me a little more than that endless paperwork. This would be a good pastime for me as well whenever I'm stuck with you like this."

His rationale seems almost flawless, particularly for someone of his character, but...

Is it truly so? Is this arrangement even acceptable? Could there really be any harm in allowing this man to delve into my case? What potential complications might arise from such a decision? In theory, there shouldn't be any problems, right...?

"But, of course, I need your permission before I start sticking my nose into your personal matters. And besides, I believe that you have already made some plans to hire someone to do the job. Am I right? Why look for someone else when a handsome and capable man is right here at your disposal?"

Her jaw fell. Really... this man...

"I don't think your handsomeness will be of any help," Eva muttered under her breath.

"You haven't the slightest idea, darling," he countered with a slow, seductive smile, savoring his wine in what seemed like slow motion, all the while never breaking eye contact. "Looks can work wonders, you know."

She couldn't deny the truth in his words. She was well aware of how the world operated; she wasn't naive about the ways of things, though she hadn't personally exploited such advantages. Beauty was undeniably a very valuable asset.

But she had honestly thought that, at the most, he would just hire some top-notch private detectives to do the job while he simply sat and waited for the information to fall into his lap. *Am I wrong? But there's no way this prince would do it on his own, right?*

"You're not seriously considering running around out there, pretending to be a detective, are you?" she asked, narrowing her eyes slightly in an attempt to discern his true intentions. But as she studied his face, she found herself unable to even begin guessing what he might be planning.

"Why not? If the need arises, I'd be more than willing to take a firsthand look. I'm expecting this to unveil some rather interesting scenarios related to these matters."

"Mr. Acheron, you are a CEO, not a detective. You really shouldn't be involving yourself in something like this."

"I'm just a CEO by name. You're the real CEO right now, while my job is just to sit back and relax," he corrected, looking quite serious. "And honestly, I don't see an issue with it anyway. I can do the job smoothly and cleanly for you, Eva. It would not even come at any extra cost, and you'd be getting good service for sure. I'm giving you my word."

A tinge of suspicion reemerged in her heart. Despite her efforts, she couldn't shake it off. She still couldn't wrap her head around why this man, who appeared so detached from the trivial aspects of life, was now ready to do everything for her.

"Fine. Since you're so insistent, who am I to deny your entertainment?" she relented, realizing that this option was preferable to the alternatives currently available to her.

Although she continued to question his motives, she knew she couldn't fully trust anyone else she might consider hiring at this moment.

Additionally, she saw the advantage in keeping Gage occupied.

This was definitely better than him disappearing on her again doing god knows what, right?

"But if you mess up and something bad happens, I will hold you accountable. You hear me, Mr. Acheron?" she told him, trying to look and sound as strict and serious as possible so that he'd know this matter wasn't just some plaything.

The corner of his lips quirked up, his eyes sparkling with that almost irritating level of confidence as he replied, "Of course you'd say that. But worry not, Eva darling. Because Gage Acheron does not mess up."

She could only sigh. The confidence of this man was just out of this world!

"You're not even asking me anything regarding this matter?" she started after a short silence. "You are supposed to ask me first if the accusations are truth or not before jumping into this."

"I don't need to—"

"Why? What if the news is right? What if I indeed committed such a crime?"

She immediately regretted her words, but it was too late. *Gods… why do I talk too much when I'm with this man?*

"Then I'll find all the evidence of your crime and burn them to ashes."

His response had her eyes circling so wide. Her jaw fell slack, and she could only look at him, utterly dumbfounded. Logic told her that this man was definitely not serious but… that look in his eyes…

No way… why would he do such a thing for a stranger like her? *I might be tripping!*

"Don't think too much about this darling," he broke the silence, reaching out to pinch her cheek but stopped midway, perhaps afraid he'd ruin her make-up. "It's not that hard for me to see who's committing a crime between you and the Youngs."

"R-really?" she probed, curious.

"Just think about it… why did the Youngs need to get rid of the goose that lays golden eggs? I don't think it's all because of that silly reason of you being just their adopted daughter. I'm guessing you've been turned into a scapegoat because someone in the family indeed committed some serious crime."

CHAPTER 19

It was already past midnight when they finally arrived at Gage's mansion.

As soon as Eva entered the door, she rushed upstairs, took a quick shower, and went through her beauty routine before hurrying into Gage's bedroom.

When she found that the bed was still empty, she sighed in relief. She hoped he would stay out until she was done warming his bed.

Damn the contract that binds me to do these weird things for him!

Unsure of what she should do, she grumbled under her breath and dove into the inviting bed. She lay down on her back and stared at the ceiling. He did not give her any rules about this, so what exactly should she do?

Should I roll my body over? Ugh! Whatever!

She huffed out and proceeded to roll about in the spacious bed.

After five minutes or so, Eva finally stopped rolling around and blushed in embarrassment.

Damn it! What the hell am I doing?

She groaned and buried her face into the pillow, absentmindedly taking note of how soft yet firm the pillow was.

And it… smelled incredibly nice. His scent was all over everything in this bed, and she couldn't help but inhale and…

Ugh! Get a grip on yourself, Eva! You're here to warm the freaking bed!

Eva shook her head. Since he did not specify a rule, she really did not need to warm up everything… *right?*

All right, I will just lie here in the middle like a corpse. That's it! I am not going to roll all over this large king-sized bed like a complete idiot.

Suddenly, she froze. Her eyes widened as she finally realized that the bloody, arrogant devil was already sitting on the chair. His long legs were comfortably folded as he watched her.

How long has he been sitting there watching me make a fool of myself?!

Eva felt like she wanted to slam her face into the pillow and scream her lungs out due to embarrassment.

"I thought you were going to roll around for another twenty minutes or more," he said, looking as though he had just watched the most adorable video clip he'd seen his entire life.

She shot him a fierce glare, ready to retort, but he suddenly stood up from the chair and removed his robe in one fluid motion. The revealing of his toned and distracting upper body made Eva forget her intended words.

When he began to approach the bed, half-naked, Eva felt her heart skipped a beat. *Wait a moment, devil…*

As he leaned over to climb onto the bed, Eva quickly stretched out her arms, palms facing him, and exclaimed, "What are you doing? I'm not done warming your bed yet."

He blinked at her innocently. *Innocently? Yeah, right…*

She rolled her eyes internally. This guy was definitely anything but innocent!

"There is no rule that I can't be on my bed while you're still warming it up, right, Eva?"

"Yes, but… it's not warm yet."

"Don't tell me…" He paused, tilting his head slightly. "Are you scared?"

"Of… of course not!" she blurted out.

"Then I'm lying down. I'm tired."

Eva automatically scooted to the other side of the bed as he let his large frame settle onto it.

Tired, my foot! Eva fumed silently. *All you did was lounge on the couch, sleep, and play with your tablet for hours!*

Not wanting to appear like she was overreacting, she focused quietly on the ceiling. Despite feeling exhausted and sleepy—undoubtedly more so than the devil beside her—she reminded herself that she couldn't possibly fall asleep on his bed!

"Come a bit closer, Eva." His deep voice broke the silence. "At this rate, you're just going to warm the edge of the bed."

"I can't touch you while I'm warming your bed, remember?"

"I remember. But you're still too far away."

With a sigh of resignation, Eva inched a bit closer in his direction.

"Closer," he said again, and she shot him another glare, only to realize his eyes were already closed.

"You're not doing this on purpose just so I'll end up breaking one of the conditions, are you? I'm telling you now, Gage Acheron, I won't fall for it," Eva firmly said, refusing to move any closer to him.

The corner of his lips curled up. "Stop overthinking things, Eva, and just relax."

She couldn't help but feel nervous. This was her first time lying in the same bed with a man—while he was in it, too. It was ironic because, despite having a boyfriend and even a fiancé for years, she had never been in a situation like this before.

There were quite a few chances for Julian to come over to her house and sleep over, but he never did, even though both of them knew the passwords to each other's apartments. This fact had never bothered her before, but now that she thought more about it, she could see all the signs that Julian was just not into her like she had thought ever since their time in college.

Was I so utterly unattractive that he never even bothered to make any advances aside from simple kisses and sending expensive gifts?

She couldn't believe how she never realized how foolish she was. She had thought that the two of them were just so alike.

She had liked Julian ever since high school, admired him, and she believed her feelings even deepened in college.

And she believed she loved him even more when they got engaged. Whenever they had their once-a-month date, he always assured her that everything was okay. That everything else could wait until their wedding. She had always acted like a gentleman toward her. He was always so understanding.

Julian had told her that she had nothing to worry about because they were the same. That the two of them were just too busy and that it was normal for them not to be engaged in any sexual activities yet. Believed that he, too, was just not interested in it yet.

The foolish her of the past had fully believed that liar and swallowed his lies hook, line, and sinker.

Now she knew that she was the only one. Julian was most probably actively engaging in sex with other women since god knows when while she did not even think about it.

That bastard!

A sudden vibration jolted her from her thoughts.

She immediately sat up.

"It's my phone. I set an alarm in case I fell asleep while warming your bed," Eva explained upon noticing Gage's confusion as he searched for the source of the vibration.

Gage looked speechless as he watched her climb off the bed.

"Well then, goodnight, Mr. Acheron."

"Wait a moment." His voice halted her in her tracks, and she turned to look at him. "Don't you think you've forgotten something?"

Eva blinked, and then her eyes widened. "Oh, right! God, I'm sorry. I totally forgot about that."

She hastily walked back. She wanted to just crash her lips against his again and be done in a blink of an eye but because Gage was already standing next to the bed, her plan was no longer possible.

Once close enough to him, she paused and then she tiptoed, expecting him to bend over because he was just too tall!

But Gage's hands gripped her shoulders.

Frowning, Eva stared at him with questions in her eyes.

"What are you doing? You can't touch me, remember?"

A ghost of an amused smile flashed across his handsome face.

"Actually, you've failed a condition, Eva. So I should be the one who would be kissing you this time."

"What…?"

126

"Footnote of the term 'every night,'" he stated in a matter-of-fact tone, and Eva's eyes circled wide again, finally remembering that the term "every night" means "before midnight" in the contract she signed.

Oh damn! Why the hell did I forget about that?!

Despite all the scolding she was inwardly throwing at herself, Eva remained outwardly calm. She could not do anything about it anymore, no matter how she berated herself anyway. All she could do now was accept the consequences.

Besides, there was nothing for her to worry about, as it was just a kiss. It was not that big of a deal. Julian had kissed her many times before when she was still with him.

"All right." Eva cleared her throat and pulled away from him, straightening her stance. "I really need to go to bed and rest soon... so please proceed and get over with it."

She shut her eyes closed.

Seconds ticked by, but he had not done anything yet. Cracking one eye open, Eva spoke. "What's the matter, Mr. Acheron? Don't tell me you're nerv—"

His face was suddenly so close to hers.

"Were you just about to say that I am nervous?" he asked, and Eva felt her heartbeat accelerate.

He is just... he is too large... too close!

The corner of his lips twitched upward. "Relax, Eva. Just breathe," he said in a smooth voice, and Eva reddened, knowing that he must be hearing the loud and fast thumps of her heartbeat right now. "I'm just going to kiss you, not eat you up, Pet."

She forced out a smile. "Right." She gave him a quick nod and then echoed the words, "It's just a kiss."

A deep breath then escaped her lips, and her business-mode look was back in just a few moments.

"All right, I'm ready. Let's just get over it now, Mr. Acheron," she declared in an almost commanding tone, causing Gage's eyes to light up with a glint of something playful.

And yet, Eva would not dare compare the playfulness in his eyes to the mischief of an innocent boy because that playful glint she had caught sent a strange shiver down her spine.

"First things first, Eva." His deep voice echoed in her ears, and her thoughts quickly scattered like spilled popcorn the moment his hot and moist breath brushed past her cheek.

Still, she managed to marshal against herself and keep her composure.

"I think I need to teach you how to kiss first."

"W-what?! You don't need to do that. I am not new to this, Mr. Acheron."

She couldn't help but glare at him.

Sure, she would not consider herself a seductress, but neither was she a first timer at kissing. She was already twenty-eight years old, not a teenager!

He shot a smoldering gaze at her.

"Just because you've been kissed before doesn't mean you'd instantly know how it's done properly, Eva."

His graceful fingers cupped around her jaw, and that one move made her forget all that she was about to say. The feeling of his fingertip behind her ear surprised her and sent her mind into a momentarily blanked-out state.

Before she knew it, her gaze was locked onto those deep and devouring eyes. They looked different again. As if the colors of his dark pupils magically changed into hazel…

"Pay close attention to what I am about to teach you, Eva," he whispered as his hand slid slowly to the back of her neck, lightly grasping to support the weight of her head. Every inch of skin he touched seemed to prickle with goosebumps. "I'll show you what a real kiss is like."

And his mouth came down on hers.

His lips were like a warm delight that she had not expected.

Gently, he explored her lips with tender pressure, exploring repeatedly like he was trying to coax her. She had thought… he was going to roughly kiss her or give her a punishing kiss, as this was supposed to be a punishment.

But Gage's kiss felt so sweet and warm that she could not help but want to… respond.

Every brush of his lips against hers kept melting, something cold and frozen within her.

This was… she had totally not expected this! *Oh no, Eva, this is… bad.*

129

Moments passed, and when Gage finally pulled away, a protest almost escaped from her lips. Her hands were tightly gripping the material of her pajamas to keep them from touching him, and they tightened even more in her effort to stop them from reaching out and stopping him from pulling away.

She thought that this kiss would be a piece of cake for her. She was quite certain that she did not find Julian's kisses bad or anything of the sort. In fact, from all the times they had kissed, she remembered that it was quite pleasant. It was just that... this man's kiss... Gage's kiss, was just so very different. It was achingly...

His kiss was doing something strange to her body... something that Julian's kisses had never made her feel.

"Let me in, Eva," came his whisper. His voice was suddenly so... so bewitching. It was as if her whole mind was now trapped in an alluring fog of his making, and she could imagine that voice belonging to a beautiful devil tempting her into sin.

She honestly didn't know how she managed to pull herself away from him and stepped back in a daze.

But Gage took a step forward, negating her earlier action of trying to put some distance between them. He was holding her gaze as if he had no plan to release her from his bewitchment. Then there came a sudden smile that flashed across his face, one that was somehow seductively wicked. But then... it was gone so fast that Eva was unsure if she had truly seen it or if it was just an illusion her own worked-up imagination cooked up from the suddenly raging hormones she was experiencing right now.

Eva continued stepping backward because he did not stop narrowing the distance that she was trying to put between them.

They continued in that manner—her taking one step back, followed by him taking one step toward her—until her back finally hit the solid wall behind her.

His powerful arms jailed her, pressing his palms on either side of her against the wall.

"W-what… are you doing, Mr. Acheron? It's done, right? You've already… kissed me. I'm now allowed to leave."

She tried her hardest to gather her wits.

He tilted his head slightly. "Nope, it's not done yet, Eva. We had just barely started… so you can't go yet." That deep voice and that look in his eyes evoked a shiver to spread across her skin.

"What? Look here, Gage. You've already kissed me so—"

"Consequence if condition 1.1 is not met," he said, cutting her off. "Party B will be the one to initiate the kiss. Party B will be allowed to kiss Party A however long or whatever way Party B wants. Party A has no right to deny Party B in this punishment," he recited, particularly emphasizing the parts "however long or whatever way."

Eva swallowed hard. She felt like she was prey that was now caught in this devil's trap. *This… this sly devil!*

131

She just really did not understand. Why did this man want to even kiss her in the first place? It had been weighing in her mind why his conditions were even like this.

"Also. Like you, I have my definition of a kiss, Eva. Yours is a punch-kiss, right? Mine is… I don't consider it a kiss if it is just the lips involved, darling. That's just a peck for me, not a kiss. So, if you want this to be over soon…" His fingertip dragged slowly over her lips, stroking at first before parting them apart. "Open this pretty mouth of yours and let me in, Eva."

Eva could not help but feel her defenses crumble, just like the sandcastles on the beach being dissolved by the crashing waves of the sea. All that happened was just him touching her lips and her listening to the sound of his voice. It was so much deeper, huskier, and darker than usual. And she could feel it weaving its dark magic through her, seducing her, luring her, hypnotizing her. She felt his long fingers slightly tighten around the sides of her face. His eyes seemed to have turned into devouring pools, and she could not bring herself to look away. She could not do anything else but stare at all that gorgeousness that was on display before her.

Before she knew it, his hand was already at the back of her neck, grasping lightly as he supported the weight of her head in the palm of his hand.

The warning bells rang louder than ever at the back of her mind, screaming at her that this whole thing was a bad idea in the first place. That letting him in was a dangerous move on her part. She should try to think of some way to maybe convince him or reason it out with him... or perhaps find a loophole that could bend favor to be on her side. But damn it!

Her mind just did not seem to be working. No... it was more like her mind did not want to work. It had gone on strike and had shut down in favor of just enjoying this heady moment she was in. His gaze, his closeness, his voice... his scent... everything about him just filled all her damned senses, and now she felt like she was now totally under his spell. Without any way out, apparently.

Fine!

She gave in. She was going to do it and get this done with. Just this once. She swore to herself that this would be the first and last time she would ever allow this kind of situation to happen again.

As if he saw and understood the surrender in her eyes, a ghost of a smile flashed across his face.

And like a predator who could no longer waste any moments in wanting to taste its prey, his mouth crashed against hers.

She opened her mouth to give him access, all the while screaming at herself, reminding herself that she should not be touching him.

"Condition #1.1: Party A must not touch Party B while kissing Party B." She recited one of the ridiculous conditions in her mind, and it seemed to have worked somewhat.

When his arm slid around her back and pulled her against him, Eva clenched her fists. She could feel the solid and unyielding body of his pressing up against hers, and she felt like her system was going awry. Then his tongue smoothly slid inside her mouth.

The silken touch shocked her, and she could no longer keep her body stiff. It was like he had put a drug in her mouth using his skillful, hot tongue that had quickly melted away all her stiff muscles.

Her plan on wanting to keep acting like a lifeless log until he was done was no longer possible, no matter how much she forced herself.

Why... oh why... how can this devil taste like... this?!

He tangled his tongue with hers, licking everywhere and anywhere as if he were planning to claim everything as his.

Oh God... what is this? Are kisses supposed to be like this?

Her head started to spin. Her senses were being overwhelmed. The sensation seemed to invade every nerve in her body, making her writhe from the undeniable sweetness. And she would not... could no longer... fight it anymore...

She kissed him back.

And when she thought that nothing could possibly be more intense than the way he was kissing her, she was proven wrong almost immediately. Because the moment she responded, his kiss suddenly morphed into something so...

Oh God, I can't even think anymore.

The slow and passionately sensual kissing a while ago turned to a whole new level as he possessed her mouth. He played, stroked, suckled, and more, until a moan had slipped helplessly from her throat. It was all spinning out of her control now. Well, if she was honest with herself, she was never in control in the first place. She had absolutely no idea, had never thought that a kiss could be like this. She never thought it could be this deep, this good, this all-consuming.

He did not seem to want to relent. His tongue explored her thoroughly, entered her over and over as if he couldn't get enough, starting another kiss before the previous one had quite finished. And she could do nothing but writhe in bewildered pleasure. Pleasure that she had never felt before.

Her hands were on his chest. They were just pressing against him as evidence of her failed attempt to push him away. She could no longer resist, even if she forced herself. Because now even her legs seemed to be losing their strength.

God… I was right all along. This man is truly… as dangerous as hell!

Then, all of a sudden, he released her, tore his mouth off hers as if someone had yelled at him to stop. She could not quite see his expression due to the haze that had fogged her eyes once their mouths parted. But she could tell that both of them were breathing heavily.

135

The first thing she realized the moment she gathered her wits was the feel of his hands steadying her. Then she saw her hands fisting on his shirt tightly.

Slowly, she loosened her grip, and suddenly, she pushed away and turned around.

Without a word and without another glance back at the man, Eva staggered toward the door and left.

Panting hard, she ran toward her room, which was not all that far from Gage's. The instant she shut her door behind her, she slid to the floor and buried her face into her palms.

CHAPTER 20

Gage remained leaning against his room's door.

A slow, disbelieving smile curved across his face before he opened his eyes slowly to stare at his room's ceiling.

His eyes were gleaming as he moved his thumb over his lower lip.

But then he sighed, and his smile faded.

"Damn… she looked so bewildered. You should've held back a little…" he muttered as he ran his fingers through his hair.

"But fuck… she's so…"

His gaze dropped to the massive bulge in his pants, and he slowly caught his lip between his teeth.

"Fuck…" he cursed again.

Finally moving from the door, he didn't head toward the bed but instead entered the bathroom.

He turned on the shower and stepped under the cascading water without taking his pants off.

But despite the cold shower, his arousal didn't subside.

Pressing one hand against the marble wall, he freed his rock-hard length and wrapped his hand around it.

He slid his veiny hand up and down. And soon, his breathing became rapid as he replayed in his mind the way she had innocently kissed him back. The way her little tongue entwined with his... the way her moan sounded.

It was insane how a single kiss from her could turn him into this, but it wasn't really surprising. This woman was his Eva, after all.

"Fuck... Eva..." he groaned as he quickened his pace, and when he finally came undone, her name echoed loudly in the bathroom.

CHAPTER 21

"Is Gage up yet?" Eva asked Eloise as she sat in front of her make-up table.

"Um… not yet, miss. He's still in bed, it seems," Eloise replied as she worked on Eva's makeup.

"That little…" Eva shut her eyes closed for a while before she continued in a calm tone, "Is he really this way every morning?"

"Er… no, Miss Lee… Actually, Mr. Acheron usually doesn't wake up late as far as I know."

When her makeup was done, and the bloody devil was still not coming out, Eva finally lost her temper and stormed into his room.

The man did not even make any move when she approached his bed with her intentionally noisy footsteps. She pulled the thick curtains open, but since Gage was facing the other side, the morning light did not seem to bother him in the least.

Sighing, Eva rushed to the other side of his bed and was about to yell at him when she suddenly halted in her tracks. Seeing his face reminded her of last night, and she…

Stop it! Eva! Damn it. Forget about it! she yelled at herself inwardly, not daring to stare at his lips.

In that moment, Eva forced herself to only think about one thing: to never let her guard down around him again. *Never again!*

This man had the power to shatter her walls without even being forceful. He did it so cunningly and so smoothly that she was genuinely afraid she might end up crumbling before him without her even realizing it.

What happened last night proved the power he had over her. And she swore to never again let it escalate to the point that they had reached last night. No. She should never let herself fall into his trap again. Because if that happened again, she knew she might never be able to break free from this dangerous man.

She cannot let that happen. She must not! She refused to fall for a man again. Not now. Especially not him. Not for this too-good-to-be-true creature called Gage Acheron.

"Mr. Acheron! Please wake up!" she yelled at him, crossing her arms over her chest.

He made a pleasant rumbling sound before his eyes slowly cracked open and looked up at her.

The corner of his lips lifted lazily. "Morning, darling."

Eva clenched her jaw at the sight of him staring at her with those dreamy eyes and that morning voice… Damn him. Attacking her right the moment he opened his eyes should be a crime!

"Good morning, Mr. Acheron. Please get up now or else…"

"Or else?" he teased, not moving an inch as he continued to gaze up at her with that damned dreamy morning look.

"Or else…" She felt her brain lagging again as she struggled to think of a comeback. "I'll tickle you until you can't breathe," she finished a little weakly as she blushed at her lame threat. She was already internally calling herself stupid for what she had just spouted.

Then his pleasant chuckle echoed.

Eva's face burned at how childish those words sounded now as they echoed once more in her mind.

But, well, tickling is indeed a good way to force someone out of bed, no?

She had heard one of her former secretaries doing that to her husband, and she said the move was very effective. So why should she not do it to this infuriating man as well? She might as well try it before he tells her to kiss him awake again!

Without warning, Eva reached out to Gage's side, pointed her finger, and poked him.

"What do you think you are doing, hmm, darling?" Gage's lazy morning voice echoed out.

She straightened her spine almost immediately like a Girl Scout at attention.

141

She looked at him only to see him smirking devilishly at her. *Darn! That was embarrassing!*

Clearing her throat, Eva quickly gathered herself. "Please rise and get ready, Mr. Acheron. We can't be rushing to work again today because that's just too tiring. Also, you are no longer a child who needs someone to wake them up every single morning. You're already an adult, so I am really hoping you will cooperate and be responsible for yourself."

For some reason, he smiled as if amused about something before he let out a lazy sigh and finally stretched.

"Did you sleep well, Eva?" he asked, resting his temple on his knuckles as he waited for her answer, looking as though he had all the time in the world to be patiently waiting for her to respond.

She looked away and stared at the window for a moment, trying her best not to show any expression on her face. "I did. Now please get up and get ready for work. I'll go get dressed now. See you downstairs, Mr. Acheron."

CHAPTER 22

Their second day at work was less hectic.

As always, Eva smoothly performed every task required of her.

She was meticulous and fast, practically like a machine when she was in work mode.

Watching her, Gage couldn't help but smile.

She did not even bother to lift her gaze to look at him, even when he was staring at her. He was being ignored completely once again.

Returning his gaze to the files he was reading on his tablet, his smile eventually faded. He then put his tablet down and threw his head back.

He stared at the ceiling and thought he might need to stall a bit in dealing with Eva's case against the Youngs. He could start now, dig up all the dirt on XY, and gather more than enough evidence.

But the image of Eva's suspicious glare as she looked at him made him smile to himself once again.

He could already imagine her growing more doubtful of him if he completed the job at what she deemed an impossible pace, and that was the last thing he wanted.

Subtly nodding to himself, he thought that it was better for him to take his time and handle it step by step at a pace she would consider reasonable.

There was no need to rush right now anyway.

On their way home, the sound of an alarm clock ringing echoed inside the car, causing Gage to look down at his wristwatch.

It was already 10:10 in the evening.

Glancing at Eva, he saw her turning off the alarm she had set on her phone. His brow raised, and a disbelieving smile nearly burst forth from his face as he realized what that alarm was for.

"It's time for my task," the little tigress said seriously before moving closer to him.

Gage was speechless.

He had not expected her to take such precautionary measures. This bloody cruel little tigress of his...

And just like that, it came again, that unceremonious punch in the lips.

"Ah... don't you feel sorry for abusing my poor lips, Eva?" he asked, smiling at her.

That seemed to throw her off a little, but she cleared her throat and retorted, "I don't think that's abuse, Mr. Acheron. I am only doing my task."

She immediately went back to her seat and returned her gaze to her tablet as if nothing out of the ordinary had happened, as though what she had done was just one of the business tasks on her checklist to be marked off.

He half-bit his lower lip before releasing it slowly.

"Did I scare you last night, Eva?" he finally asked, his eyes focused on her.

She paused.

"Of course not," came her straight reply, her tone neutral despite the blush at the tips of her ears. "It was just a kiss. Why should I be scared?"

The car stopped before Gage could respond.

Eva quickly grabbed the car door handle and hastily got out, while Gage just sat there watching the little tigress run away from him.

He could tell that she was being extremely cautious of him now. And with all those alarm clocks she had set on her phone, he knew that his smart and cautious little tigress would never forget her task again.

As he stepped out of the car and watched her small back enter the main door of his mansion, an expression that looked like a half-smile and half-challenge flashed across his face.

CHAPTER 23

After showering, Eva hastily rushed over to Gage's room.

She breathed a sigh of relief when she saw that he was not there yet and once again wished that he would not join her in his bed like the last time. It was easy for her to ignore him when she was working, but here in his comfortable and warm bed, it was hard to do the same.

Gage had a way of drawing any woman to him, even when he was just sitting there. He was the type of man who could make any woman beg for his attention, his love, his everything. And that was the type of man she never wanted to have anything to do with. She did not want to fall for any man.

Not right now, and again, especially not Gage Acheron.

Yes, he had been nothing but nice to her. But Julian had also been an angel to her for years. Though Julian had never been as attentive as Gage, he had also been nice and gentlemanly before that night. Julian had taught her the bitter and cruel reality that no matter how nicely someone treated her, it might be nothing but a facade.

Eva did not want to open her heart and trust anyone again. At least not for now.

She did not know when she would willingly open her heart again, but she had planned not to until she got her absolute revenge. And that would obviously take a long while. If she were to be realistic, it might take a long time.

She was so sure of herself that nothing could distract her from her goal.

Nothing would. Until Gage kissed her last night. That one mind-blowing kiss was enough to make her realize that it only took one wrong move and she might end up as prey, completely at Gage's mercy.

So, she was going to stand her ground. He had said it himself that as long as she could perform her task, she had nothing else to worry about.

"Relax, Eva." His deep voice echoed in the quiet room. "I don't want you lying there in my bed like I'm going to do something... bad to you," his dark and lazy voice floated over to her.

Eva shot him a strict glance, only to see him leaning against the doorframe, looking so... so handsome as hell! His relaxed stance, with his hands crossed over his chest, those tousled damp hairs covering part of his beautiful eyes, the way he stared, the way he breathed...

oh damn it! This man is definitely doing this on purpose, right?! He is clearly trying to seduce me, right?!

She couldn't believe she was actually so easy to sway. This had never happened to her before. *Gods... why did he have to be this handsome and perfect, and... why couldn't he be just a normal, average guy? I wouldn't be having such a hard time right now if he didn't look so attractive, right?!*

Secretly taking a deep breath, Eva forced herself to relax. "I think it's impossible for me to relax when lying in a man's bed. So do bear with me, Mr. Acheron," she said in a clipped tone.

Her whole body tensed up once again when he moved and walked over.

"Hmm..." he hummed, slowly approaching her.

But the closer he got to her, the less her heartbeat sped up.

It was... strange.

She had worried he'd hear how loud and fast her heartbeats were as soon as he reached her because she was expecting her heart to actually act crazier the closer he got. But for some reason, her nervousness was suddenly subsiding instead.

Was it because everything about him seemed less extreme right now?

Well, except for his appearance, something about him felt quite low-key tonight. It was hard to explain, but she wondered if it had something to do with the fact that he hadn't teased her at all today or approached her too closely and looked at her with that certain devilish gaze of his.

He sat on the other side of the bed, stretched out, and lay down next to her.

She watched him shut his eyes as he breathed out.

"I honestly want to prove you wrong right now. But knowing you, you'd probably punch me in the face for real, not with your mouth, but your fist this time if I tried anything," he spoke so casually, with a small smile on his face.

"It's good that you are smart enough to realize that." Eva nodded.

He let out a short, amused laugh. Then he turned to face her.

Eva didn't like it because it felt quite overwhelming for him to lie there, facing her. She quickly fixed her gaze on the ceiling, daring not to let her eyes wander in case they drifted back to him again.

"Why… I mean… is there a reason why you want someone to warm your bed every night?" she asked. She needed to fill the awkward silence, or she might start getting nervous again.

"Hmm… it makes me sleep better."

"You mean you can actually sleep without someone warming up your bed first? I actually thought you couldn't at all, and you might even have some kind of condition or trauma about it. Well, I have read and heard stories about chronic insomnia and other sleeping disorders. And this usually occurs among businessmen and top executives like

149

you… So this doesn't really sound weird to me at all," Eva chattered on.

She waited for his response, but nothing came, so she was forced to turn to check, only to see him already seemingly asleep next to her.

Eva's brows creased. *What?! That could not be, right?! How could he be sleeping already? This man… he must be feigning sleep, right?! I am not going to fall for such…*

She blinked. She stared closely at his eyes. The movement of his eyeballs and those shallow breaths… *S-seriously? Is he truly asleep?*

Eva could only stare at him, mouth slightly parted. She was really at a loss for words. She never thought he could actually fall asleep that quickly.

She allowed her eyes to drift closed and let out a soft sigh. Why was she even thinking so much about this? She was tired and sleepy as hell herself because of the mere few hours of sleep she had last night.

Opening her eyes again, she stared at that ridiculously handsome face that was even more so now that he was asleep.

Her eyes were getting heavier. *What a face… how can he be so handsome?* Before she knew it, she was touching his face. *Darn… When will my alarm clock go off?*

CHAPTER 24

When Gage felt Eva's hand, which had been lightly touching his cheek, finally dropped to the bed, he slowly opened his eyes.

He had decided to feign sleep so she would finally relax. He couldn't stand how tense she was.

It was clear to him now that she was determined not to let what happened last night happen again, and he wanted to punch himself because he knew this was the result of what he'd done.

He should have really held back a little, no matter how hard it was. But he lost control. The moment she opened her sweet lips and let him in, he just lost it.

Her mouth was heaven.

She was heaven.

Her kisses were to die for, and he would definitely risk anything to have a taste of her again.

But here she was now, so nervous, so cautious, and it was all his fault.

"You need to get a hold of yourself, you idiot," he muttered to himself, sighing as he stared at her sleeping face when her alarm clock went off, vibrating at her side.

When she didn't wake up by the second vibration, he carefully reached out and turned it off.

"Since you've once again failed a condition—touching me while you're warming my bed—I will use the corresponding punishment request for this. You are now to sleep here in my bed tonight," he whispered as he pulled the heavy comforter up and silently covered her.

He did not want to disrupt her sleep, so he scrapped the idea of carrying her back to her bed. They had slept together once already, so he thought this wouldn't make her come at him like a tiger tomorrow. She wouldn't be bothered about this, would she? Well, probably.

His gaze softened.

"You work too hard, Eva. Way too hard. If you insist on keeping this up, you will only end up breaking yourself," he commented in a low voice, then sighed, retracting his hand that was about to touch her soft cheek.

For a long while, he didn't look away. He simply watched her peaceful face. *Fuck... I want to touch her... hold her... kiss...*

He bit his lip as he caught himself staring at her delicious mouth.

Taking a deep breath, he turned away and stared at the ceiling for a few moments before he quietly and slowly rose and left the bed.

CHAPTER 25

The sunlight spilled warmly through a crack in the curtains, but Eva lay frozen in bed. Her hand was draped over a solid, hard torso that she knew belonged to no one else but Gage. The wonderfully pleasing scent of his was something she could never mistake for someone else's.

What in the world had happened?! How did I end up sleeping in his bed and even hugging him?! And my alarm?! What happened to my goddamned alarm?!

She couldn't help but scream at herself. Did her blazing determination to keep her distance from this man just get defeated by sleep?!

Oh, gods...

It was unbelievable because she knew what she was like. She could pull all-nighters and still never fall asleep just anywhere if her mind refused to. Yet here she was...

And Eva! You are like a baby koala clinging desperately to its mother! Get off him now before he wakes up and sees this embarrassing situation you've put yourself in! her inner demoness yelled at her, and her face turned so hot she felt like she was going to explode from embarrassment.

But before she could even lift her arm, Gage moved.

She stiffened.

And when his arm covered hers, she caught her breath. The timing of that movement seemed a bit… It was as if he was trying to stop her attempt to escape from his grasp and his bed!

Eva tried to push his arm off hers, but he was as immovable as a stone. She knew he was huge, but she never thought his arm would be this heavy.

It must be because he is still asleep, right?

Relieved that he was still sleeping, she took a deep breath and tried again. This time, she did not hold back and pushed with all her might.

ARGH! What on earth does he eat? Cement and rocks?! How can he be so damned heavy?!

Suddenly, he tightened his arm around her, pulling her closer to his chest in one quick move. The unexpected action took Eva by surprise.

She tilted her head up, ready to launch a tirade at him, but ended up catching her breath instead.

His face was so near. And she couldn't help but stare at his features. His flawless skin, long lashes, thick brows, and…

She quickly looked further down to avoid staring at his lips. However, what greeted her sight next were her palms splayed on his solid and very drool-worthy chest.

Oh, gods!

His heat, his steady and strong heartbeat transmitted directly to her palms, and his warm breath puffed into her face…

She shook her head, afraid that if this kept up, she might actually end up relaxing in his embrace.

No, damn it! Eva! You must not! Work… work! You have to work! You need to get up. Now!

Eva pushed at his chest, but he was not budging. She felt like she was chained completely in his arms, with no escape unless he let go.

Left without a choice, she reluctantly called out his name to wake him up.

"Mr. Acheron, w-we nee… need to get up now," her voice broke the silence.

He didn't open his eyes but responded with a rumbling "hmm" before falling silent again. That sound tickled something inside her, and for a moment, she stayed still, waiting for him to make that sound again. *Damn… what the hell is wrong with me?*

"Mr. Acheron… please!"

When he still did not open his eyes, Eva finally called out his name a little louder, just short of shouting at him. "Gage!"

At last, he eased his hold on her, but only just enough for them to be able to look at each other.

His lashes finally fluttered open, and Eva momentarily forgot everything else when their eyes met.

Were his eyes always this hazel? She thought they were black during the day, but now they looked different during daylight too?

She shut her eyes tight and when she looked again, the colors were back to black, causing her lips to fall open. Damn it... why are her eyes seriously playing tricks on her at a time like this?

"Yes, darling?" were the first words he said. The nonchalance in his expression and tone had her reeling in utter disbelief.

How could he be behaving like this?

Here she was, flustered and overwhelmed, going almost batshit crazy at how close they were and with the sudden kinship between them. And here he was, acting as if there was nothing amiss with their current situation. Like this was all totally fine, as if this was an everyday occurrence he had long gotten used to.

This didn't make sense to her because they had just met a few days ago and weren't even in a romantic relationship!

"You... you really are trying my patience, aren't you?" she hissed. If she were a cat, she would have all her claws brandished and fur standing up, hissing and spitting in agitation. Actually, his handsome face might even have claw marks already.

She wanted to head-butt him so badly because he was being annoyingly calm and even seemed to be enjoying himself at her expense.

He lifted an elegant brow at her, then pressed his forefinger on the deep lines that had formed between her eyebrows.

"You really turn into a tigress the moment you wake up." He sounded amused. "You were like an adorable, clingy, and furry kitten while you were asleep," he added, patting her head.

"You turned my alarm off last night, didn't you?" she cut him off, narrowing her eyes accusingly at him.

"It rang twice, and you didn't wake up so…"

Eva bit her lips at his explanation. She knew she was tired as hell yesterday, so it was indeed possible that she couldn't wake up at the sound of her alarm.

"You should've woken me up then," she muttered, still unhappy.

"Why should I, hmm, Eva? You want me to kick a tired little kitten out of my bed? True, I don't claim to be a saint. But I wouldn't go so far as to do that. Especially when it's you."

Why did he have to add those last four words?! Now, she was getting all flustered again.

Damn this man and his sweet mouth! *No… I need to stay strong and focused! I must not fall for his words!*

"Waking someone up is not the same as kicking someone out of bed, Mr. Acheron," she somehow managed to retort.

"It's pretty much the same thing to me, Eva. Waking you up means I'm kicking you out of my bed."

157

Eva could only sigh and then shut her eyes before drawing in a deep breath. There was no use in arguing with this sly devil. She just knew she could never win against him! He would always have the last say! It was always something that would either make her jaw drop or make her face flush beet-red if she tried to retort or one-up him.

"Fine, fine! Whatever you say. Just let go of me now," she surrendered with a sigh.

"Ah, how cold you're treating me. After you have used me so selfishly, like I'm your personal human pillow and heater all night, this is how you're going to get rid of me?"

"W-what? What the hell are you saying?! P-please stop making up stories like that—" Eva stuttered.

"Gage Acheron does not make up stories, Eva. I guess… for evidence purposes, I should probably take a photo next time."

She could only blush to her roots again. She knew that she loved hugging pillows when sleeping in bed, and that was why she had multiple bolsters at home.

"There won't be a next time, Mr. Acheron. Now please let go," Eva insisted, swearing to herself that she must never allow something like this to ever happen again! Never!

However, the devil still did not move.

Eva sighed heavily in surrender.

"Fine. I'm sorry. It won't happen again," Eva could only apologize, knowing she needed to give in if she wanted to get out of his bed and finally start their day.

If this kept up, she might actually lose her temper or end up wasting her precious energy so early in the day. And she did not have the luxury to dilly-dally like this. She had lots of things to do today—things that were important. Way more important than bantering endlessly with this handsome devil.

Though this man was important, he was just her second priority. Her first priority was her job and ACEON!

"I don't want a verbal apology. I want compensation, Eva. There should always be give and take in exchanges to be fair, don't you think?" Gage bargained.

Why in the world is he suddenly bargaining now?!

"And no. I won't be accepting another punch in the lips this time," he stated his condition when he caught her eyes darting to his lips, causing her to clench her jaw in embarrassment.

"Then what do you want?" she asked a little aggressively, still embarrassed that he caught her thoughts on just brushing it off with a kiss—a kiss that he termed a punch.

She couldn't help but grumble internally, telling herself that her kisses were definitely not bad enough to be considered a punch.

She kissed relatively well, okay?!

"A minute-long kiss from you would be enough," he said generously, as though he was giving her a discount.

"Five seconds," she negotiated assertively.

159

A minute-long kiss with this man was nothing but plain bad news to her. She would rather work overtime than engage in a minute-long kiss with him! She had learned her lesson already!

"Not a chance, Eva," he disagreed.

"Ten seconds."

"You can't possibly think I would be okay with that. You have gained hours on me. All I'm asking for is a measly minute. Is that really too much to ask?"

"Fine, thirty seconds."

He bit his lower lip, then closed his eyes, acting as though he did not hear her.

"All right. I guess you still need more time to think about it. I'll sleep for thirty more minutes."

"Fine! Oh my God! Gage, you're—" Eva choked up at how agitated she was.

There was no way she would win when haggling with this man! *He is truly worse than a fishwife!*

He immediately rose, shocking her at how quickly he moved.

And damn him for looking gorgeous even with his messy morning hair.

"Now then—" He bent over, but Eva stopped him, placing her palms against his broad chest.

"W-wait a moment!" She raised her voice a little as she pushed at him. "I haven't even brushed my teeth yet!"

Before he could say a word, she frantically climbed off the bed as if the house was on fire.

Thankfully, he did not try to stop her anymore. He just sighed audibly and combed his fingers through his hair.

"I'll collect my kiss later then, darling," he said charitably before he finally got up and headed off to his bathroom.

CHAPTER 26

All day long, Eva was immersed in a new project proposal. It was a project that would directly compete with XY Corporation's flagship product, so Eva was intensely interested in it and determined to secure the deal. She was so hellbent she worked nonstop with a demeanor that practically screamed, "This is the chance I've been waiting for!"

When nighttime came, Eva finished all her tasks without any problems. She punch-kissed him and then warmed his bed, this time without falling asleep. Well, it was because she had set her alarm to the maximum volume.

Gage did not try to tease her because he could tell it would not be possible to pull Eva's full attention to him. Her mind and heart were fully focused on nothing else but her plans for vengeance—that project she believed would be just the thing to kick-start her plans for the downfall of XY.

And so, just like that, another day had passed.

Eva maintained her intense focus. Vengeance truly fueled the tigress in her, and Gage could do nothing but watch. He had been royally ignored by her for days now, but he didn't mind. There was just something so incredibly fulfilling about watching her sit there like a fiery warrior, waging her battles with intense focus. Watching her like this, a fierce tigress on a mission, was something he'd never get tired of.

"Such a workaholic woman," he muttered to himself, smirking as he ran his fingers through his hair. "Fine. I'll let you work in peace for now," he continued, keeping his gaze locked on her while she worked so seriously at her desk. "I'm not sure how long I can behave myself, though. But I will try," he added, talking to himself.

"Are you saying something?"

At last, she lifted her face to him. The lines between her brows appeared as she regarded him with a questioning gaze.

"I said you look pretty hot when you're on fire like that." He flashed his seductive smile at her, leaning his shoulder against the wall.

Her eyes widened for a moment, but just as he thought he finally managed to have her attention, she suddenly scowled and returned her focus to her work, once again acting as though he did not exist.

"That's my little tigress…" He chuckled quietly. "I bet she doesn't even know she's the only one who can ignore me like this." He then sighed in amusement. "So work is my biggest rival here... huh..."

CHAPTER 27

A week later...

Eva felt incredibly thankful that Gage had been remarkably good over the past several days. He hadn't given her a hard time at all, especially with their arrangements and the conditions of the contract.

It had shocked her at first because it was unusual for the mischievous man to suddenly stop pestering her and start behaving so perfectly, like a good boy! He had woken up early without her nagging, and he didn't try to tease her either.

For some reason, he had been so cooperative that she genuinely felt grateful. In fact, he was so amazing she even considered it a blessing to work with such an understanding and outstanding boss!

For the whole of last week, her schedule had been beyond hectic. She couldn't imagine how the week would have gone if Gage had continued with his unreasonable and mischievous antics. Instead, he had been a great help.

Because of his supportive interventions, she didn't feel as overworked as she had expected, despite the crazy deadlines she had imposed on herself. Gage had been simply reliable the whole week and had been the total opposite of what he had claimed to be—lazy as hell.

He had stepped up in ways she hadn't anticipated. Whenever she needed assistance, Gage was there, offering his expertise. His unexpected support allowed her to stay focused and energized, even when the workload seemed overwhelming.

Gage's transformation from her mischievous tormentor to a dependable partner had been nothing short of miraculous.

She found herself wondering if something happened or if there was some hidden agenda behind his sudden change of behavior. Regardless, she appreciated his cooperation more than she could express.

Now, here they were on their very first business trip together. This was also Eva's first official trip since she had been kicked out of XY Corporation, so she was honestly excited.

"I don't think we need two rooms, Miss Lee," Gage said nonchalantly as they entered a hotel in La Defense, the major financial district of Paris.

Eva glanced sharply at him, narrowing her eyes. "I disagree, sir. We are not a couple. You are my boss, and I am your secretary," she replied sternly but with Evelyn Lee's friendly and discreetly sweet smile.

He leaned in closer, whispering, "Are you sure about that, darling?"

Eva felt goosebumps as his hot breath touched her ear. She hadn't seen that coming! He had stopped teasing her for the last seven days, and now that he was suddenly doing it again, she couldn't help but react strongly. Thankfully, she managed to maintain her composure and refrained from glaring or scolding him, especially with people around watching them.

"I am very sure, sir. I have never been surer of anything in my whole life!" she answered in clipped tones, smiling as professionally as she could while internally grumbling. *I need to have a stern word with him ASAP so he won't do that again!*

"Then don't blame me later," he replied, a quick smirk tugging at his lips.

That smirk gave her a bad premonition.

As they approached the front desk, Eva took a deep breath.

"Good evening. We have a reservation under Acheron," she said to the receptionist.

"Yes, welcome, Mr. Acheron and Miss Lee," the receptionist replied, typing into the computer. "We have you booked in two deluxe rooms. Will that be all right?"

Eva was about to nod when Gage leaned over the counter and spoke.

"Actually, we'll just take one room, please. Preferably with a view."

Eva's eyes widened, and she quickly interjected, "Two rooms, please. As originally booked." She turned to Gage, her gaze firm. "We agreed on two rooms."

Gage held up his hands in mock surrender, his eyes twinkling with mischief. "All right, all right. Two rooms it is."

The receptionist smiled. "Of course. Here are your keys. Enjoy your stay."

As they headed to the elevator, Eva sighed. The mischievous devil was back. *Why now? Can't he just behave like the perfect man he was just moments ago?*

When they were inside the elevator, Eva turned to him and smiled professionally. "Let's just get through this trip without any more of your mischievous antics, okay, sir?"

"No promises," he said, winking at her as the elevator doors opened.

Once they stepped out of the elevator, Gage headed in the opposite direction. But he stopped and turned around to look at her over his shoulder. "Well then, Miss Lee. See you tomorrow," he said, flashing her that smirk again before he strolled away.

Eva just stood there, watching his retreating figure. Somehow, that uneasy feeling she had earlier resurfaced after seeing his smirk. It was like she was forgetting something very important.

What is it? What is it?!

Gage's smirk kept flashing in her mind. She knew there must be something he knew that she was forgetting.

Then it popped into her mind. *The contract! The condition! My task!*

If she wanted to keep the peace and focus on her work, she could not possibly give him even a hint of a reason to start messing with her again by breaking any of his conditions! This sly man!

"Wait! Sir! Mr. Acheron!" She immediately rushed after his retreating back.

To her surprise, he did not stop at all. *This insufferable big devil!*

"Gage!" she shouted out, red-faced.

He halted immediately.

"Hmm?" He looked over his shoulder innocently, pretending to be shocked that she was running after him, all flushed and panting. She gritted her teeth, all the while cursing him in her mind.

She took a deep, stabilizing breath before saying, "You're right. I guess we won't be needing two separate rooms." Eva spoke coolly, "Let's go, sir."

Gage half-bit down on his lower lip as if trying to stop himself from smiling before he nodded amiably.

He led the way to his presidential suite, clearly pleased with the turn of events.

Eva, on the other hand, followed with resignation.

When they reached the door, Gage tapped the key card and held the door open for her. "After you, Miss Lee."

Eva stepped inside the place where they would stay for three nights.

The suite was lavish, with modern decor and a breathtaking view of the city skyline. It had all the luxury she would expect from a top-tier hotel. But there was a huge problem! There was only one bed!

Gods… I seriously forgot about the fact that there would be only one bed?! What the hell is wrong with me?

Hastily, she walked over to the phone and called the reception.

While she was on the phone, Gage settled himself on the comfortable sofa, facing a floor-to-ceiling window that overlooked the beautiful city.

"They said there are no other rooms available and that the room you just canceled is already taken," Eva reported as she approached him. "I can't believe my room is already taken. It's just been a couple of minutes since you called!"

"This hotel is extremely popular, after all. And before you suggest it, nope, we won't be wasting time looking for another hotel, Eva. This is the best hotel in the area. And you should know that I only expect the best in everything. So forget it," Gage said, casually rejecting Eva's unspoken idea of finding another hotel while keeping his eyes on the sunset.

Eva sighed, realizing there was no easy way out of this situation.

She fell quiet and did not protest anymore as she eyed the comfortable and large sofa with much thought. "I'll go take a shower first," she said, then left quietly to get their luggage.

But just as she grabbed their bags, Gage took them from her hands and brought them next to the closet, arranging the bags neatly to the side. Eva then dealt with her luggage and arranged it in the closet.

Once she was done, she stared at Gage's. Deciding that it was no big deal for her since she was his assistant after all, she opened his luggage and started arranging his things in the closet as well.

She was his personal secretary, and she knew this was part of her job description, too. She didn't mind doing this at all, but somehow, looking at their clothes being arranged and placed inside a single closet felt a bit…

Eva shook her head to clear it of any unnecessary thoughts before quickly rushing into the bathroom for her bath.

Later that evening after their dinner, the duo worked silently, and then afterwards, Eva finished her task by punch kissing him without warning while he was busily reading a file from his tablet.

The devil did not complain at all though and just simply continued working after her punch kiss.

When she was done with her bed-warming duty, she rose to leave the bed when Gage's voice echoed out. "You're not going to sleep on the sofa, Eva. I will not allow it."

She spun around to look at him and found him gazing at her as he lay there, half-naked from the waist up. If she had not steeled her mind and been ready for it, she was sure that her face would have flushed red from the sight.

For many nights, she had tried not even to glance in his direction while warming his bed. Of course, it was all to avoid looking at such a wonderful scene and the temptation it brought. After all, she was apparently just like every woman when it came to this man.

"And no, I'm not going to be a gentleman and give you my bed either," he added flatly, his tone uncompromising. "You and I will sleep right here in this bed."

She pressed her lips tightly together for a moment before responding. "Look here, Gage. I am not going to—"

"You have nothing to be afraid of, Eva," he cut her off, not allowing her to finish. "I'm not going to touch you without your permission. I'm not that type of man, in case you're still having doubts."

Eva could not help but bite the inside of her lower lip. Hard. Of course, she knew that already! If he was that type of a man, she would have been a goner since the first night she had slept in his bed. By now, she was not even worried about him at all! What she was worried about was herself! She was just trying to put herself in check because she had already found out that she had this inexplicable weakness when it came to his touch and kisses!

Distraction was the last thing she needed at these crucial moments. She found any romantic relationship or affair a massive distraction to her and her work. And that was why she tried so hard to stay away from him. No matter what it took.

"I know that," she muttered.

"Then be a good girl, lie down, and go to sleep. I won't do anything to you," Gage told her as he waved to her side of the bed.

"But… but I might do something to you!" she finally blurted out with eyes wide and cheeks burning. She instantly regretted saying that at all, of course, but it was too late.

"That's not a problem with me. I don't think you'll do anything other than turn me into your personal pillow anyway," he replied rather casually, rendering Eva speechless. "So stop taking everything so seriously and sleep. Now, Eva."

That look in his eyes had her unable to protest anymore. So, she could only listen and lie down, turning her back to face him. Well, he was right. There was nothing to worry about since she would be dead asleep anyway, right? She would not even remember whatever she would end up doing to him.

Her eyes quickly became heavy. She did not know why, but she seemed to always fall asleep so easily when she was next to him in bed.

"Must be just coincidence…" she told herself before she finally drifted off into dreamland.

CHAPTER 28

At last, the first day of their business trip was over. Eva was pretty amazed at Gage the entire time he was dealing with his business partners.

He was actually an incredibly amazing and charming CEO, if not the most charming businessman she had ever seen.

She could not help but wonder what trick it was that Gage was hiding for him to charm everyone so easily like that.

At the same time, she could not help but feel a little mad that he was not actually that interested in the job he was so good at!

"Thank you." Eva smiled at the stylists as they finally finished her make-up and everything.

Upon stepping out of the dressing room, she saw Gage sitting there, wearing a sleek, tailored black suit that included a vest under the jacket and a silver-gray tie that matched the color of her dress.

Gage was invited by one of the most powerful businessmen in the city to attend his birthday party tonight, and she, of course, was going as his plus-one for the night.

"Beautiful as always, Miss Lee." He smiled as he regarded her.

"You sure this isn't too showy?" Eva asked, a bit worried as she fiddled with her dress. She was wearing a stunning, shimmering silver sleeveless gown with a V-neckline and a high slit on one side.

"It's not too showy at all, Eva," he whispered reassuringly in her ear once he approached her. "You will be surprised to see how you'll still be one of the most decently clothed at the party tonight. Still easily the most stunning, too."

Eva flushed a little at his last line. She still could not get used to his praise, even though she should be used to it by now because Gage had always been such a polite man. She had seen multiple times how smooth he was in praising others and making everyone feel good.

"Thank you, sir," she replied, accepting his outstretched hand.

Soon, they finally arrived at the party's location. It was a luxurious castle at the top of a hill.

Just as Eva was about to take Gage's hand to leave the car, she suddenly stilled. Her eyes widened as she looked through the car's window.

"So that's Evangeline Young's ex-fiancé and sister, huh?" Gage commented casually, causing Eva's gaze to fly to him and saw him looking at Julian and Jessa passing their car.

The corner of his lips lifted up. "Let's hang around here for a while."

She frowned a little, wondering what he was up to.

As though he had read the questions in her mind, he continued, "Let's just say I feel like stealing the show tonight."

Minutes passed.

"Gage, I think it's about time we head in," Eva broke the silence. "We are already fifteen minutes late. Our tardiness might end up becoming a blow to your reputation, and I don't want that happening."

"Relax, darling," he replied, still looking so annoyingly carefree. "I'm guessing you must have been that girl in class who was never late."

"You are right. I don't do late. And that's because I don't like unpunctual people."

"You must have had boring school days, then."

"Huh? Why would you assume that my school life was boring just because I am always punctual?" Eva had never thought her school life was ever boring. Learning was exciting to her, especially reading.

"Hmm… I shall show you the fun of being late, Eva. Just wait for it." He flashed that devilish smile again, rendering her speechless.

Several more minutes later, they finally stepped out of the car.

The two of them walked slowly and gracefully toward the luxuriously decorated entrance. Eva wanted to quicken her pace, but the man had a firm hold on her as if he knew that she would have run off if he did not grab on to her.

"Relax and just go with the flow, okay?" he whispered into her ear. Eva thought to herself that since they were already late, she would just let it go for once and allow him to take the lead on this.

Once Eva nodded, they finally entered, her hand curled around his arm.

Gage had stopped a waitress who was coming out of the hall and took two glasses of champagne from her. A small frown flashed across Eva's face for a while before she smoothed her expression and accepted the glass Gage was offering. She held her tongue, did not ask any questions, and simply held on to his arm again.

As expected, the entire hall screamed with extravagance. Eva guessed that approximately fifty thousand or more LED lights were used to decorate this entire hall. The dance floor was also dazzling and simply... over the top.

The welcome speech was already over! And seeing that everyone was already holding on to their glasses meant they were about to make the welcome toast. *Oh goodness! We are super late!*

The birthday celebrant, who was already on stage, caught sight of them immediately.

But contrary to what she was expecting, the old billionaire, Mr. DiMarco, only smiled welcomingly at them and lifted a hand in greeting.

"I am very glad you made it in time, Mr. Acheron," the birthday man greeted on the mic, causing everyone to turn their heads to the back to see who the distinguished guest was that even the host had to acknowledge.

All eyes were on them now.

And Eva did her very best to stay composed. She was really embarrassed at all the unexpected attention. It was almost like they were the ones celebrating their birthday and stealing the show!

This is definitely not okay, Gage!

Mr. DiMarco then lifted his glass, and everyone, including Gage and Eva, lifted theirs, too, for the toast.

After that, once everyone was seated, Gage smoothly led her to the table arranged for them at the front-most row where the VVIPs were seated.

As they walked in front of everyone, Eva could feel the multiple gazes—she sensed many curious, but a few seemed jealous—boring into her back.

And then they passed in front of Julian and Jessa.

Eva did not know if it was intentional on Gage's part, but they slowed down as they walked so elegantly before them.

Gage suddenly leaned closer to her and whispered, "Anything bothering you, darling?"

"I'm good. I was just wondering what I should do if Julian suddenly decides to approach us. I think he has definitely recognized me, Gage."

"Hmm... you sure about that? I don't think that the idiot recognized you..." Gage replied.

Her brows pulled together for a moment before she quickly faked a smile, remembering that she was attending as her new persona, Evelyn Lee, tonight. "Are you sure?"

"Stop thinking about him or them and just focus on me, darling. Even if they did recognize you, they wouldn't dare approach you and make a scene in this place."

"Well... you are right."

"Though... since he's an idiot, he might. But I am here for you. So just relax and enjoy yourself." Gage lifted his glass and nodded at her with that devilish smile plastered on his face.

Soon, the dazzling dance floor was filled with couples having a good time.

When the music slowed, Gage stood and offered Eva his hand rather chivalrously.

Eva, of course, did not hesitate to accept his offer, and thus, the two of them waltzed off toward the dance floor.

"Your ex keeps throwing glances your way, Eva," Gage whispered close in her ear as they danced.

Raising a brow, Eva glanced to her side, but it was not Julian she saw first. Jessa came into her view, and she was staring at... Gage.

This little... is she serious?! How can she look at another man with eyes like that while dancing with her own man?

Eva shut her eyes and took a deep breath. Then another fake sweet smile tugged at her lips as she tried to gather herself.

"And Jessa is staring at you, do you know that? I can even hear her thoughts already," she told Gage in a low voice. Though her lips were smiling, the tone of her voice changed slightly.

"That's interesting. Do you mind telling me what this Jessa's thoughts are about?"

"Maybe coming up with an elaborate plan on how to hit on you later."

"Hmm... if she does try to hit on me, are you going to let that happen and just watch from the sidelines, darling?"

Eva's brows knitted, and suddenly, she forgot about her facade and glared at Gage. His question had immediately put numerous unwanted thoughts into her head. If she did not do anything to stop Jessa, would Gage reciprocate once Jessa really made a move on him? Was he going to fall for Jessa's charm just as Julian did? Would she welcome Jessa's advances?!

Her grip on him suddenly tightened, and she did not know why she had dropped her head. She hated this. She hated how her heart and mind were in such turmoil right now! Because... when it comes to matters such as these, her confidence was really low. She did not know how to charm men.

Was this dread that she was feeling coiling low in her stomach? Was she afraid that Jessa would take Gage away from her and...

Her imagination took over and went into overdrive. All the possible future outcomes once Jessa took Gage flashed across her mind one after another in a dizzying array of scenes that caused her heart to shrivel up bit by bit. She imagined that Gage would then revoke their contract, and she would get kicked out of his house and her position as his personal secretary. She would then not be able to execute her revenge on the Youngs, and Gage would then...

"Eva." His cool and minty breath that literally touched the insides of her ear jolted her back to reality. He was so close to her that his lips were almost brushing against her ear.

"What in the world are you getting into a tizzy for, huh? Little tigress?"

Eva pulled her head away to stare at him, her eyes still containing traces of her dazed condition from earlier.

"You..." Her expression suddenly turned fierce. "If you get yourself charmed by Jessa and dare to revoke our contract, I will... I'm going to... going to... to bury you alive, do you hear me?!"

Gage's pupils dilated before he bit down on his lower lip as if to stop himself from grinning.

Bending closer, he moved his lips so close to her ear again and whispered in a mischievous, seductive voice, "I would fucking love it if you bury me… deep inside you, darling."

"W-what?" Eva stammered and blushed so hard that her speech was starting to fail her. "Y-you… really… h-how could y-you…"

She couldn't believe she was now stammering like a teenage schoolgirl. Damn… the longer she spent her time in the company of this… this devil, the more she would splutter!

He chuckled quietly after pulling her closer to his body and continued dancing.

"Stop thinking about your sister, Eva. Didn't I tell you to focus on me alone? Don't ruin the moment by overthinking, okay?" he whispered again. The mischief in his voice was now gone. All that was left was his mesmerizing tenor voice filling her ears.

"I can't help it. Jessa is very charming and beautiful… just like you," she said helplessly, turning her eyes away from looking at his.

Though she did not want to admit it, she still said it. It was a fact to her that would not go away even if she denied it.

"Oh… really? I think I'm very much offended, Eva. How could you even compare me to her?"

"What…?" Eva looked at him, confused.

"She is not even close to you."

When her frown deepened, Gage was about to speak more, but the dance finally ended.

He bowed smartly at her, and she curtsied beautifully at him.

Just as they were about to head back to their table, Julian and Jessa blocked their way.

"How about an exchange of partners, Mr. Acheron?" Julian offered rather gentlemanly.

But Eva ignored him as her gaze was fixed on Jessa, who was busy making that innocent angel-like face before Gage.

"May I have this dance with you, Miss…" Julian offered his hand to Eva.

"Evelyn Lee." Gage was the one who answered for her.

Jessa, on the other hand, was shamelessly staring at Gage with desire in her eyes.

Is something wrong with her head? Julian is standing right next to her, and there she is, acting like a dumbstruck fool towards another man?!

She was never close to Jessa. In fact, she barely even knew her because both of them had been distant from each other.

Eva had also been sent abroad and spent most of her time overseas. When she came back home, Eva had been too busy with her work, and Jessa also did not bother about her. Despite being sisters by name, Eva believed that the two of them did not know each other well at all.

"Mr. Acheron, may I have this dance?" Jessa's sweet-as-sugar voice echoed as she reached out in an attempt to hold Gage's arm when…

Eva suddenly stepped in between them, pushing Jessa's hand away lightly just before she could touch Gage.

"Apologies, Ms. Young. But Mr. Acheron is off-limits," Eva said boldly, her tone clipped and stern.

Jessa's face twisted, her innocent facade crumbling. "What do you mean he's off-limits? Don't tell me… is Mr. Acheron actually dating a mere secretary like you?" she sneered at Eva.

"No," Eva instantly replied. "Mr. Acheron is not dating his secretary. However, he's already taken, and his lover has asked me to watch over him and keep dangerous women away from him. Therefore, my apologies again, Ms. Young."

"Do you think we are blind to see how intimate the two of you were since the moment you entered the hall? I personally think Mr. Acheron's lover should be wary of a leech like you, miss secretary."

"Ah, that's because Mr. Acheron's lover trusts me, Ms. Young. And this is supposed to be a secret… but it seems that I will need to spell everything out for you." Eva leaned in a little bit closer to Jessa and whispered, "Our intimacy is actually all part of an act. It's just our strategy so that any sensible woman would stay away from him. But it seems you, Ms. Young, are not among those sensible women, are you?" Eva tilted her chin up slightly at Jessa.

"How dare…" Jessa barely stopped herself from blowing up. "And what makes you think that I would believe any words that come from a mere secretary?" She looked at Gage, and her expression instantly changed to something so innocent.

"Mr. Acheron, why don't you say something?" she added with a voice that could convince anyone she was the victim, and she did nothing wrong.

Eva stilled, shocked.

Her heart started to thud intensely.

Damn it, Eva! Why did you say those things? Where did you even get the courage to spout all that nonsense in front of Gage himself?! Could you not think of a better way?! her inner demoness yelled at her.

She knew she had gotten carried away… There was no way Gage would support all her lies, right? Why should he when, clearly, she was the one making things up without even consulting him?

Eva could already imagine, seeing it clearly in her head what would happen next. Because she couldn't remember the last time someone was on her side when Jessa and she were in situations like this.

When she was truthful, no one stood by her… How could she expect anyone to side with her over Jessa now when she was the one lying?

"Actually," Gage started before pausing for a moment, and Eva found herself holding her breath, expecting the worst, "Miss Lee is right. I am indeed taken."

Eva's eyes widened in shock and disbelief.

His unexpected answer made her world come to a standstill before she finally breathed again.

Then she felt a warm sensation filling up her heart… her entire being.

When he subtly winked at her in a conspiratorial manner, a tingle worked up from her toes and all the way up to her scalp.

"No, no… you're lying, Mr. Acheron. You're just covering up for your secretary!" Jessa's voice pulled Eva's attention from Gage.

"Well, whether I am lying or not, I don't owe you any explanation." Gage eyed Jessa from her head down to her toes with what seemed like an uninterested and bland gaze.

"Who do you think you are? Do you even have a say in anything I do?"

Jessa froze, utterly shocked.

Eva, too, actually. She had not seen that coming! She did not know Gage could be so savage!

And before Eva could recover from her surprise, Gage whispered to her and told her they were heading back to their table.

But as she followed after Gage, Eva stumbled.

A hand grabbed around her waist from behind, catching her from falling forward.

Gage immediately turned, and Eva swore that his face seemed to have darkened at the sight of Julian holding her. *What's with that look…?*

"Are you all right, Ms. Evelyn?" Julian's voice echoed in Eva's ear, but she was yanked away from him before Eva could react.

Totally ignoring the duo, Gage's arm wrapped possessively around Eva's waist, supporting her as they walked off.

CHAPTER 29

While Gage was with Mr. DiMarco and the other CEO's and big personalities a short distance away, Eva sat in their table quietly. Her mind was occupied, still thinking about what had happened earlier. It was the first time she had felt fully supported like that by someone, and she hadn't anticipated how it would make her feel. She didn't know it would feel like this!

This was the first time that someone chose her side over Jessa's, and to think that she was the one lying this time. The feeling was… just indescribable for her.

Thinking back, she was so used to always being the one at fault and had to bear all the scoldings. She was always the one on whom the blame fell. Between her and Jessa, her family and everyone else had always sided with Jessa, whether she was right or not.

Ever since she was young, no matter what she did, she had not felt her family truly cared. Even if she was not their child by blood, they should have at least given her some attention. But they had not bothered. All their love was poured out wholeheartedly onto Jessa. And Jessa… greedily took it all.

Eva remembered that day when she had once received a gift from one of her aunts when they were still children. Jessa had wanted it even though she already had a mountain of gifts. Usually, she would relent and hand over the things Jessa wanted without putting up a fight. But that one time, Eva really liked the gift so much that she fought for it. Jessa had forcefully snatched it from her and then burst out crying, bawling to their parents that Eva had hurt her. She ended up being scolded harshly and was slapped by their mother. She still could not forget the scorn on her mother's face that day. For so long, she wondered if it was normal for a mother to look at her child like that. Only now, she understood. It was all because her mother never considered her as her own child.

Taking the glass of wine sitting in front of her, Eva drank it in one gulp. She kept staring at Gage, who was currently being occupied by conversation with Mr. DiMarco and some other high-profile CEOs. She could see that mischievous devil charming them again with his impeccable conversational skills.

Earlier, Gage had led her back to their table and sat down with her when Mr. DiMarco walked over and invited Gage to join him and a few other VIPs for a private talk. Eva had urged Gage to go on and join them because she knew how important it was for businessmen to never miss these kinds of opportunities to make connections. That was why she was now sitting there alone at their table.

Everything was fine so far until she spotted Jessa among the group of CEOs right next to Gage.

Getting the waiter to pour her another glass of wine, Eva forced herself to relax. She should not feel this riled up. This kind of scenario was not even that surprising. This was perfectly normal. She had been there and done that previously as the ex-CEO, and during the past few days, Gage had even dined with a couple of beautiful superstars with whom they had chosen to collaborate on a commercial for their brand.

She had never felt this bothered, even when she saw how those ladies acted so touchy-feely with Gage. So why was she having a hard time keeping her cool today? Why was she this affected when Jessa was now involved?

"Mind me joining you, Miss Lee?" a male voice pulled her out of her thoughts.

The familiar voice made her pause for a moment, but she lifted her gaze anyway, only to realize how close Julian was as he sat next to her.

"Our partners are busy right now, so I think we should hang out while we wait for them. What do you think?" He smiled. That gentlemanly smile she was so used to seeing for years… A smile that she had foolishly thought was one that was genuine and full of his sincere feelings. *Ha! What a joke!*

Eva almost scoffed but managed to restrain herself.

Outwardly, she still maintained her passive and neutral expression as she ignored him and simply continued sipping on her wine.

"You know what?" his smooth voice echoed again. "I somehow keep getting the feeling that I've met you before, Miss Lee."

Eva nearly choked on her mouthful of wine. But she managed not to show the surprise in her face. She recovered nicely and only blinked at him blankly a couple of times.

"You're probably the sixth man who has already told me that, Mr. Park," Eva lied rather smoothly, raising an elegant brow at him.

Julian did not look offended or annoyed. In fact, he chuckled in good humor.

"Well, some men do overuse that line quite a lot. So, I understand if you doubt its credibility. But I am being serious here, Miss Lee. You seem really familiar to me…" he commented and rubbed his chin in contemplation.

"Familiar…" Eva echoed, her voice sweet and delicate. "Well, maybe we have bumped against each other at some other business events before?"

"Hmm… I don't think it's just one event, though."

Eva's hand, which was holding on to her glass, halted in midair.

Her heartbeat quickened at the thought that Julian might have already realized it was her and was actually just pretending now.

191

Still smiling, he added in a light voice, "I keep being reminded of my college sweetheart while looking at you."

Eva's heart nearly stopped. This man had definitely recognized her and was just pretending... right?

But she tipped her glass and finished the rest of her wine while using the time to think about how to respond to his comment. Her mind was reeling when her phone vibrated before she could open her mouth to reply to him.

Eloise? Why is she calling? My stylist never calls without a prior message!

Eva looked at Julian and found the perfect opportunity to escape for the time being.

"Excuse me, Mr. Park, but I need to answer this." She stood and elegantly strode away toward the garden.

"Hello? Eloise?" Eva asked. But then the line was suddenly cut.

Curious, Eva was about to dial Eloise's number again when she received a text message. It was Eloise apologizing because she had accidentally dialed the wrong number.

Eva could only blink. Was this really a coincidence? Somehow, her gut told her there was more to this, but whatever it was, she was thankful as it gave her the perfect excuse to escape Julian.

Shaking her head, Eva sighed and headed to the bathroom. She needed to calm down and get herself as composed and clearheaded as possible in case Julian was still waiting for her back there. She must watch her words. Even if he was suspicious, or even if he already knew, there would be no way for him to confirm as long as she would not admit anything.

Upon leaving the bathroom, Eva was shocked to see Julian standing there, leaning against a wall, seemingly waiting for someone.

When their eyes met, he smiled at her.

Eva walked past him. But he followed after her, causing Eva to halt and turn around to face him. "Some ladies might not mind, but I find such stalker behavior a major turn-off, Mr. Park." Eva did her best to behave and sound like Miss Lee—confident, sexy.

"I went to the bathroom too, Miss Lee. I saw you entered the ladies' room, so I waited for you. After all, we can accompany each other back to the ballroom, right?" he replied calmly.

A female's voice pulled at Eva's attention, and the moment she turned, she froze.

Gage was right there, looking at her—at them. And Jessa was leaning against Gage's chest.

Everything seemed to suddenly move in slow motion.

And all Eva could do at that moment was watch as Gage grabbed Jessa's shoulders, moved Jessa aside, and walked past her.

Gage's gaze was sharp, spine-chilling, as he strode forward. He still looked calm, but something cold seemed to lurk in his eyes.

Eva could almost feel a heavy pressure as he got nearer to them. But when he finally stood before Julian, Gage did not say anything. He simply trained his gaze on Julian, a gaze that felt so utterly cold.

But the moment he shifted his eyes to her, that seemingly deadly look was gone. As if she'd simply imagined it earlier.

He bent over, moving his upper body closer to her than was necessary. "I was looking for you, Miss Lee," he whispered in her ear. "Something urgent came up, so we'll need to leave the party early. Now, let's be on our way, shall we?"

CHAPTER 30

"What's wrong, little tigress?" Gage's voice echoed inside the limo.

Eva tore her gaze from the car's window and looked at him. He had his long legs crossed as he leaned back casually in his seat, those gorgeous eyes of his staring intently at her.

"Nothing. I think the wine got to me a little," Eva replied simply before looking away from him again. "What urgent matter suddenly came up, Mr. Acheron?"

Gage did not respond for a few moments, but she could feel his gaze still on her.

"Come closer, Eva."

Goosebumps suddenly covered her skin.

"W-what?"

She frowned at him, even as her ears reddened.

"I said come closer."

Eva's breath nearly hitched at those words. Something dark yet warm wove through his deep voice, and God… it

195

was as if there was something in him right now that was compelling her to want to obey his command. His voice… his eyes… they seemed to be trying to pull her toward him…

And now she didn't know what to do… didn't know how to react. When did she start feeling so overwhelmed just by him talking to her like this? And what was with him suddenly commanding her while looking at her so hypnotizingly like that? *Can he stop playing around with me?*

"How stubborn." He sighed, smiling slightly. That intensity in his eyes seemed to subside a little.

Then he leaned over and reached out for her hand.

A mischievous but serious gleam danced in his beautiful eyes as he asked, "Are you jealous, darling?"

"What?!" she exclaimed. The word "jealous" had her heart almost jumping out of her throat. "Why would… what's wrong with you?"

Feeling aggrieved that he was teasing her again, she shot him an angry glare.

The car swerved sharply.

Eva gasped as her body jolted sideways with the abrupt motion.

The moment the sound of screeching tires stopped, Eva found herself already sitting on his lap. His arms tightly wrapped around her waist, securing her.

Wide-eyed, Eva looked at him.

"Apologies, sir. A rock has fallen on the road," the driver announced.

Eva couldn't help but whip her head toward the driver. *S-seriously?!*

"I see…" Gage replied, and the driver raised the partition again.

Eva pushed against him so she could return to her own seat, but Gage did not let her go.

"Tell me what's wrong first, darling, and I'll let you go," he whispered, his warm and minty breath fanning over her neck.

"Stop calling me 'darling.'" She wanted her voice to come out like a hiss. But sadly, it came out shaky and unsure. Being in this man's embrace was even more potent and heady than drinking a few glasses of wine! And that was why she really needed to get out of his arms now!

"What you saw a while ago is not what you think," he started explaining. "That particular scenario with Jessa Young is most probably a calculated move by her rather than an actual accident. She followed after me when I went to search for you. Then she walked past me in haste before turning around without warning and bumping against me. Thus resulting in what you saw."

Eva's lips parted, utterly speechless.

He did not need to explain that to her… why did he…? Oh, gods.

She never expected him to explain. And she knew he never needed to. Yet here he was…

She couldn't doubt the truth of his words. Not only because she knew that Jessa indeed loved doing such things… loved to scheme to get what she wanted… but also because she just felt he was not lying.

It was hard to explain. She knew she shouldn't just believe anything he said so easily, but… was it the look in his eyes right now?

"No, of course not. Why should I get jea… jealous? You're not mine or anything like that anyway…" Her sentence faded off as she flushed. Hard.

Forcing herself to regain her composure, which was completely falling apart, she changed the topic. "I just… I just can't stand that scent. Her perfume on you makes my head ache."

A flash of a heart-stopping smile graced his face.

"I actually feel the same. I couldn't wait to reach the hotel to take it off, but now that you said you don't like it as well…" He shifted and leaned back, spreading his arms. "Take my coat off now, Eva. Get rid of her scent on me yourself."

Those words echoed in her mind as she stayed there, just staring at his gorgeous face. And as her heartbeat began to thud louder… she obediently reached out and fisted her hand into Gage's coat.

Eva did not know what had gotten into her at that moment, but she desperately wanted to rid him of that scent! In fact, she wanted to rip his coat off and throw it out the window!

Before she realized it, her hands moved, stripping the coat off him.

Gage simply stayed still, docilely allowing her to push, pull, and lift his arms as she attempted to remove the article of clothing from him.

He did not make any move to assist her or make it easier for her to take the coat off.

What he did do was bite down halfway on his lip as if concealing a slight smile.

He gazed at her face, looking as though he was secretly having so much fun.

When she was practically hugging him while adamantly tugging at the long coat he was sitting on, "Do I really need to ask you to lift that ass of yours, Mr. Acheron?" she blurted out rather aggressively and stopped tugging, brows in a tight knot as she looked at him.

Gage lifted a brow in response, but his eyes gleamed with something else. Something... almost too hot.

"What can I do when you're seated on me like this... pressing down on me... Hmm?" His deep voice seemed to rumble like a velvet wave in her ears.

Suddenly, awareness crashed over her.

Her eyes widened as the realization of their position dawned on her lagging brain.

But she did not scramble off him. She went completely still, only looking at him. Her face turned a vivid shade of red.

Gage wrapped his arms around her, pressing her upper body against his. And then he slightly lifted himself along with her.

"Now pull on it, darling," he whispered temptingly in her ear. His lips were so close they touched her earlobe, breathing air inside.

Eva could not believe the shiver that one touch had elicited from her entire body. *Oh, gods...*

"Eva?" he called out her name, and she finally tugged at the coat under him.

Her hand was still fisted in a tight grip on the coat when Gage settled himself on the seat again. He did not release her, though, and she could not make herself pull away.

Damn it all, but... everything is just...

The coat fell from her limp hand without her even realizing she had let it go.

"Do you still smell her scent on me?" Gage asked.

His question made her realize that a hint of Jessa's scent still lingered on him. Had Jessa managed to slip her arms around Gage's waist, too? Was that the reason not only his coat that had been smeared with her scent? That seemed to be the only plausible explanation she could think of.

"It's still there," she told him.

"Then take my shirt off too, darling."

The smile Gage flashed her as he said those words could only be described as one that was pure temptation.

"Or are you going to let that woman's... scent continue clinging to me like this?" His voice was so deep, almost like the devil's whisper, tempting her to sin. His eyes were molten, bright, and smoldering as he held her gaze, compelling her to extend her fingers.

Eva reached out for his collar and fumbled with his necktie.

When the necktie fell to the floor, she reached for the button at his neck.

She was focused once again, serious as hell, as she worked intently on her task.

Once she had successfully undone the last button, the edges of his dress shirt fell open, revealing his fine and drool-worthy torso.

Slowly, she lifted her eyes, tracing the perfection of his form upward until they settled on the most dangerously compelling aspect of him: his eyes.

Those orbs of his burned hot with something resembling approval—though she was not quite sure—causing Eva's heartbeat to jump into her throat once again and drum up a crazy rhythm that had her feeling lightheaded. It was as if the dark fire in his eyes had ignited something deep within her, and... and her body started to... burn.

As she finally pulled the shirt off him, her breaths were already sounding labored.

She couldn't believe that she was already like this when all she did was remove his shirt!

"Good girl," he whispered breathlessly, and the shirt slipped from her hand. He raised his hand to her face, his finger brushing a wayward lock of her hair off her temple and gently tucking it behind her ear, his eyes never leaving hers. "You're sweating a lot, Eva."

All she could manage was to lick her suddenly parched and dry lower lip.

What… is he doing to me?

She found herself unable to look away or climb off him, even though she knew that was what she was supposed to do.

"Damn," he cursed under his breath, "did you have to lick your lips right in front of me like that? Now I desperately want to kiss that pretty mouth of yours, darling." He murmured these words as his face came so close to hers that his moist, minty breath caressed her lips, reminding her of the taste of his mouth from their intense kiss that night.

And before she knew it, her breath had become ragged and choppy, beyond her control, while he held her face and moved his lips closer.

He is going to kiss me!

She did not know what was going on with herself anymore, but…

She wanted it. She craved it. His lips against hers. His kiss.

"If you don't want this… don't part your lips," he whispered, rasping in her ear.

Then his mouth pressed against hers.

Oh… God… I'm… doomed now… right? she uttered in her mind as her lips helplessly opened up for him.

Gage pulled away and stared deep into her eyes. He looked surprised that she opened up so easily like that. But his eyes quickly burned into a dark, hot inferno, and he latched on to her mouth with a hot, searing kiss.

And just like that, the tendrils of desire quickly infected her, compelling her to throw caution to the wind and respond with abandon.

She gave in, pressing back into his kiss.

An electrifying bolt ran through her when his supple, smooth, and tantalizing tongue entered her mouth.

Eager to experience that sensation again, she mimicked the movement and returned it to Gage. Her response only served to ignite the flames into a blazing one, sending both of them into a passionate and wild kiss.

Soon, they were gasping, nipping, and licking, lost in the moment. Eva plunged one hand into his thick mane and gripped a fistful of his hair, pulling him closer.

"Oh, Eva… what a fast learner you are…" he panted out before he again claimed her mouth.

He dove deeper, making pleasurable vibrating sounds inside her mouth that sent delicious tingles zipping straight to her core.

When their lips parted the second time, they were both breathing hard.

Eva felt like her brain was fully seduced. There were no other rational thoughts in her mind anymore, nothing but this… pleasure. It was just so unlike her, but his lips, this kiss… why was it so… addictive?

And then, without warning, she made the first move this time and kissed him again. She kissed him with such abandonment that she pressed his head back against the car's headrest.

But the next time their mouths parted, he held her shoulders down, preventing her from kissing him again.

Her eyes circled at what he did, confused.

"That's enough for now, Pet," he said between his still heavy breaths, "unless you want me to completely let loose and take you right here, right now. Do you have any idea how much you've aroused me already, hm, darling?"

When she furrowed her brow, Gage bit down halfway on his lip again. Then, suddenly, his large, warm hands moved to encircle her waist and pulled her down against his... massive bulge.

A gasp escaped Eva's lips.

She felt as if her entire being had just experienced a pleasurable jolt.

Oh, gods...

"Don't look at me like you can't believe that I'm hard... you wicked little tigress," Gage said with a throaty chuckle, shaking his head. "Do you have any idea how hot and ravishing you look right now? You always do, but..." He caressed her cheek with the back of his fingers. "Tonight, you are just so... extraordinarily wild and beautiful that I can barely stop myself from..." He trailed off, clenching his jaw as if struggling for self-control.

Their gazes held.

Neither of them moved. The electric charge in the air seemed to thicken, and the car's temperature continued to rise.

Eva could feel that hot bulge nudging right against her core. She was wearing only silk panties under her dress, and the sensation of him against her was enough to set her entire body aflame.

She couldn't believe how her body was reacting at that moment. It felt unbelievable that she was experiencing these intense sensations just from being pressed so intimately against him.

Oh, gods…

She felt herself pulse against him, and a strong urge welled up within her, compelling her to grind against his hot, rock-hard length for more friction.

But then his grip around her waist loosened.

"Darling…" His voice, hot and echoing in her ear, carried a tone she had never heard before. It was raspy, gravelly, and sinfully enticing. "You should really consider getting off me soon. Like… right now. Because if you don't…" He paused. And it seemed her eyes were being tricked again as that ring of hazel appeared once more around his pupils… gleaming through his enviably long lashes, smoldering and scorching her with a dark intensity he had never shown her before. "At the count of three, you need to get off me, Eva… one… two…"

Eva heard warning bells at the back of her head. But dear God… they were so faint, so weak that they would not even be enough to awaken her from the spell she had fallen into.

That sensation, which had seemed to electrocute her when he pressed her against his erection, sparked a burning curiosity within her. She desired to feel more of it.

At that moment, something had changed within her.

For the first time in her life, she felt an indescribable and undeniable urge to experience sex. While she had, of course, thought of it before, the desire had never been this overpowering, this intense. Before, her thoughts about experiencing sex were driven by nothing more than curiosity. But now, it was completely... different.

She had come to realize now that she was truly... indeed, a woman capable of feeling the flames of lust. Yes, since the night Gage had kissed her, she had understood that she was not asexual as she had once thought.

"Three..." That one word had her breath hitching in her throat. Her lips were suddenly so dry she licked at them once again.

"Oh, damn it... Eva..." He half-laughed, half-cursed under his breath as his hold on her waist suddenly tightened once more. And then he ground her against him, startling her and causing her to moan out loudly as she shuddered in his grasp.

Her eyes flew wide as they both stilled after her reaction. She had moaned. Oh my God...!

But... she also wanted him to do that particular move again. To make her feel that sensation again.

The usual wicked mischief in those eyes of his was nowhere to be found. What remained was a searing fire, so intense that she felt as though his flame was igniting a fire within her, raging through her entire body and reaching her very core.

"Are you sure about this, Eva?" he asked in a tightly controlled voice as if someone was torturing him. "You're not... drunk, are you, my little tigress?" That last line seemed a little harder for him to say.

She couldn't stop herself from responding so fast. "I'm... not," she uttered, shaking her head vigorously from side to side.

Before she fully realized what she was doing, she took the initiative, grinding herself down against his hardness. And this time, it wasn't just her who made a sound of pleasure; he did as well.

Another ripple of sweet sensation ran through her. The feeling was so, so good that she could not find the right words to explain it. Gage's moan just now... it was... it sounded so hot in her ears. It might as well be the sexiest sound she'd ever heard in her life.

Wanting and dying to feel more of these new, mouthwatering sensations and to hear that sexy sound of his again, Eva moved her hips once more. Maybe the wine had erased any trace of her shyness, but at this moment, she hardly cared about anything else. All that was running through her mind was that she wanted more... more of this.

She felt Gage's hand cupping the back of her neck before pulling her down and kissing her again. He kissed her deeply until she felt as though her body was about to melt in his arms. His other arm held her close to him, molding her against his firm body.

She helplessly clung to him, her hands moving around of their own accord, caressing his taut muscles as she continued grinding her hips against him. She was desperate for more friction, desperate to feel more of this addictive pleasure.

Until Gage suddenly held her hips in place and backed up from their intense kiss. "You're going to drive me crazy, Eva." He chuckled softly. Then he pulled away fully from her, putting more distance between their bodies.

Eva stared at him a little begrudgingly, not liking the loss of their bodies' contact.

Her expression had Gage's eyes gleaming with amusement. "Don't worry, darling... there is no way I am stopping now unless you ask me to," he whispered as he brushed her red hair back and gathered it behind. "I want to do more sweet things to you... my little tigress."

He pressed his lips on her throat, causing Eva's eyes to slightly widen.

His mouth started kissing down her neck, planting butterfly kisses at first until he began to lick and suck her skin in earnest, sliding lower and lower.

A new wave of heat began to blossom inside her, and she writhed against him, unconsciously gripping his hair as she arched her head back helplessly and exposed her slender neck to him.

Gage's lips continued traveling downward. He then pulled her up against him, making her kneel on the car's seat with him between her spread legs. His hands began to move from her waist and then up to her breasts.

The moment he touched her mound, Eva gasped out at the shocking sensation.

He pulled away and gazed deep into her eyes. He looked like he was waiting for her to stop him from doing what he was about to do.

"Should I stop?"

Eva frantically shook her head.

He smiled, so visibly pleased at her response. Then he kissed her throat again, all the while resuming what his hand was doing.

"Relax, darling…" he whispered, and then she felt her breast being freed from her dress.

Oh, gods!

Her hands flew up to cover herself. Her face was so red as she looked at him in embarrassment.

"Did I… go too far?" he asked gently.

"I… I… I'm…"

He smiled at her. "It's fine," he whispered into her ear.

His hand around her was coaxing her gently. "You don't need to force yourself if you feel that you're not ready yet. We're not in any rush, Eva. I'd rather have you take your time," he reassured her.

"N-no, I'm… I'm old enough to be ready," she replied.

Gage blinked in silence before he bit his lip hard, suppressing a smile.

"Then… why did you…?"

"My… my breasts are… not that… they're small," she said weakly. She knew that many men preferred their partners to have large, full breasts, so she was self-conscious as she had once overheard some ladies saying her breasts were smaller than the average. Back then, Eva didn't care one bit. But now, here she was, suddenly becoming incredibly self-conscious.

Her reply seemed to silence Gage for a while before he held her shoulders and pushed her off him to look at her face. There was disbelief in his expression.

"Damn it, Eva, what did you just say?" he asked, a disbelieving smile tugging at the corner of his lips.

Eva looked away, face still blazing red, as she continued covering her breasts. "Mine are… smaller than most… women's. It's… really…"

Gage caught her wrist, and in one swift, smooth move, he lifted both her hands off her breasts.

Eva's face burned even redder with embarrassment as she opened her mouth to protest when she was suddenly tongue-tied at the look in Gage's eyes.

He stared at her breast with the kind of hunger that sent Eva's mind into a lag, like a computer that was under a virus attack.

"Your breasts are perfect, darling," he told her. "Damn, you really don't have any idea… these…" He paused before licking his lips as he hungrily ogled her twin mounds, looking as though he was staring at a mouthwatering, delicious delicacy that he could hardly wait to devour. "These breasts of yours… I'll kiss them every day until you believe how perfect they are for me," he added, and his mouth latched perfectly onto her nipple.

A gasp was torn from Eva. Her body stiffened.

As if he immediately noticed her reaction, Gage eased and returned his lips to her mouth. He kissed her passionately again, his hands caressing her back, wordlessly coaxing her. He was so patient and gentle and… just so… sweet…

"Relax, darling…" he whispered again, smiling against her lips as his mouth trailed down once more. His lips were so hot, melting her like butter under the sun.

And before Eva knew it, she was all relaxed in his arms again.

Gage took his time and patiently kissed his way to the naked tip of her breast.

Soon, she was shivering in pleasure. When she did not freeze up when he kissed her nipple, he continued his gentle ministrations.

He started toying with her now hard and wet bud, licking and skimming across it softly until Eva could no longer suppress the small sounds that were escaping from her throat.

211

"Yes, darling… just relax and let me make you feel good," he murmured. His warm breath puffed over her moist and cool peak. Then his mouth closed over it, making Eva catch her breath.

Gage sucked lightly and then twirled his tongue skillfully over and around her hard bud until she started stuttering out his name.

"G-Gage… gods…Gage…"

But when he began to gently tug at her nipple using his teeth, she tried to pull away, whimpering and quivering in his arms. She was so shocked and unnerved by all these feelings and sensations she was being driven to right now that she did not know what to do.

Gage held her close, took her hand from his forearm, and moved to place it over his chest. "Touch me, darling… Go ahead and touch me all you want," he whispered in a deep, gravelly voice. Oh, gods. His voice… sounded so erotic in her ears.

Eva's palms slowly but shyly caressed his skin, finally exploring his body. When she hesitantly moved her hands downward, Gage shivered a little.

While her hands wound their way back to his hair, he cupped her breasts and started massaging them with moderate strength as his mouth continued on his erotic attack.

And the moment her trembling fingers ran down his back and then over the slope of his shoulders, Gage purred.

Oh, that sound…

She didn't know a male sound could be that erotic… that beautiful…

Hearing his purr and moan was like hearing the most intoxicating music. Music so magical and mind-numbingly good that it sent shivers and goosebumps all over her skin, seducing every part of her being and leaving her utterly spellbound.

And she wanted nothing but to hear it again… hear him purr and moan again.

As his gentle, patient, and delicious ministrations kept on, she moved her hips against him. It elicited a sexy moan from him, and she did it again. Loving the sounds she was hearing and dying for the pleasure that seeped through her core. *Gods… it's so good… so good…*

"Patience, darling," he uttered in a tight voice as he reached out and held her tightly around her waist, effectively stopping her from moving any further.

She whimpered and buried her burning red face into the crook of his shoulders. "Gage…" She could only call his name. Her brain was completely scorched. All she could think about now was this unbearable feeling running rampant within her that she wanted to be fulfilled at all costs.

So, despite her embarrassment, she started kissing his neck, copying all the things that he had done to her.

"Please…" she cried out weakly. Gods, this lustful need…

She had never thought it would be this unbearable.

Gage groaned, and his hands finally moved to her legs. She was about to move her hips against his again but stopped at the feel of his hands crawling up her thighs.

Slowly, he moved his hand even deeper between her legs. She did not shy away this time. She instead quivered with anticipation.

When his palm cupped her through her panties, Eva's breath hitched in her throat.

Gage paused and looked up at her with those dark-bright eyes filled with gleaming starlight. She was biting her hand as she gazed back at him, her lashes damp.

"I'm going to pleasure you here next, Eva... with my... fingers," he told her, and she felt herself pulse against his hand.

She nodded without hesitation, causing him to smile with pleasure.

"Kiss me, Eva," he asked, and she obediently did as he had said.

Her mouth came against his, and she kissed him with abandon as Gage started to touch her eager and pulsing softness.

She was already dripping wet for him.

He started caressing and rubbing her through her panties until she was moaning into his mouth.

Oh, gods... please...

She wanted more. Wanted him to touch her more so desperately that when she felt him nudge her panties aside, she shivered in anticipation.

He jerked his hand off her, and before Eva could protest, he covered her with his jacket that was on the floor.

Then the car's door opened.

"Close the door. We'll be out in a minute," came his order, and then she heard the sound of the door closing.

Eva felt like a bucket of ice had been thrown all over her.

They had arrived, and it appeared neither of them had noticed. *Oh, damn it... what am I doing in a place like this? Have I totally lost my mind?!*

"Eva?" Gage held her shoulders, pushing her gently off him.

Utterly embarrassed, she buried her face in her palm.

He did not move for a few seconds before she felt him reaching for the hidden zipper of her dress.

"Let's fix you up first, darling," he whispered before he carefully tugged her dress up and covered her exposed breast.

He was so careful and gentle in attending to her that Eva slowly put down her hands and looked at him.

Once he was done, he met her gaze and smiled at her. He reached out and wiped the corner of her lips with his thumb as if trying to erase something. And then realization immediately dawned on her.

Oh, damn... my makeup!

Wide-eyed, Eva scrambled off him.

"Cover yourself with this for now, Eva," he said as he draped his jacket over her head.

215

Eva came out of the car first, making sure that her face was covered.

When she turned to look at Gage, she saw him about to come out half-naked. She felt her face getting so hot that it was as though blood would be seeping out of it soon.

Pushing him inside rather forcefully, Eva whispered loudly at him, "Please put on your shirt!"

"Oh…" He raised a brow. "But didn't you take it off me because of its foul scent?"

"Just put it on, Gage. You can't possibly be parading yourself out here half-naked like that!"

"That's not a problem for me."

"Gage!" she exclaimed.

"All right," Gage gave in, chuckling softly. "I'm putting it on. So don't cry right there, little tigress."

"Who's going to cry?!" she retorted, and Gage leisurely put on his shirt in amusement.

Eva literally ran ahead of Gage as soon as the elevator opened. She rushed to their door, and the moment she was inside, she made a beeline to the bathroom and locked the door behind her. She was so… so flustered and embarrassed and in utter disbelief… of herself. She had never thought she would ever let go and behave that way.

As she stood under the shower, letting the cold water fall on her, Eva could not get the things they had done out of her head. She remembered how wanton she had become in those moments. It was even hard for her to believe that the woman inside that car was the same Eva.

She could not recognize herself!

And Gage... Oh, gods... Would she still be able to act as usual around him from now on? What should she do now?

They were supposed to only have a boss-and-assistant relationship.

Eva spent a long time in the bath until a soft knock echoed.

"Eva?" Gage's voice rang out. "Sorry, but I need you to finish your bath as soon as possible. I mean right now, if possible. There's an emergency, and we're going home immediately."

Wide-eyed, Eva turned the tap off and rushed to dry herself. She knew from Gage's tone that whatever this emergency was, it was something serious.

Eva came out in a matter of minutes and found Gage by the door. He was busy tapping away on his phone, and his expression was... very serious.

"Let's go," he said. "I'll have someone collect our things."

Once Eva reached him, Gage grabbed her hand as if that was the most natural thing he could do at that moment. They walked quickly out of the room, hand in hand, until they entered the elevator.

"What... what happened?" Eva asked nervously, her embarrassment now completely forgotten.

Gage had pressed for the rooftop, so Eva immediately realized that they were going to take a helicopter. This only meant one thing: something really, really serious must have happened.

He glanced over at her. His expression was unsettlingly calm, and barely any readable emotion was on his face. "They said Grandpa is dying."

Time seemed to halt for a moment before Eva shook her head in denial.

"That... that can't be... he was so healthy just the other day," Eva uttered.

Gage squeezed her hand. "Don't worry, he'll be fine. We just need to get there as soon as possible."

CHAPTER 31

Utter relief flooded Eva as soon as she saw George Acheron. The chairman was awake and well, smiling warmly at her as he lay there in his hospital bed.

Last night, Eva had overheard that the chairman had been rushed to the ICU and was reportedly in critical condition. So, seeing George looking all right filled her with a mix of relief and confusion.

Could there have been a mistake? Was there some misinformation last night?

After greeting the chairman and exchanging a few words, Eva met Gage outside his grandfather's room.

"I'm so glad he's all right, Gage," she said in relief once they were alone and far enough from the guards stationed by the door.

"I told you he'd be all right, didn't I?" Gage replied.

She noticed that his expression was relaxed, so Eva thought that the chairman was truly fine. He would not be so laid-back if his grandfather was really unwell.

"But… Gage, last night I overheard that he was in a critical condition. Was that a… could there be some form of miscommunication somewhere?"

Her curious question had silenced Gage for a moment. "Kind of," he then replied rather succinctly, causing Eva to crease her brow. "Anyway, I need you to accompany him for a while, Eva. I still have his personal nurses under investigation, as there have been some shady things that may have been the cause of his collapse last night. My guess is someone messed up his medication on purpose."

Eva's eyes widened at that statement.

"He's fine now," he quickly reassured her. "He just needs to stay here for a little while longer until the result of the investigation is in. So, I'd like you to remain here for now while I'm away. You simply need to keep him company since the old man really likes you. And don't worry about the doctor and nurses who will be attending later, as the previous ones have all been switched out—these new ones were all handpicked by me. They would never try anything funny."

Eva sighed in relief.

The fact that Gage seemed to have already thought of and pre-emptively dealt with everything within this short period of time made her feel both amazed and relieved at how reliable and efficient he was. She did not mind staying back and watching over the chairman, of course. He was truly nice to her, and she was comfortable talking to him. In fact, she had loved that time they had their tea together.

If there was something she could do for the chairman, then she would do it.

"Leave him to me, Gage. I'll make sure to watch over him and keep him company," Eva said determinedly, causing Gage to flash her an approving smile.

"Are you going over to deal with the investigation?" she asked.

He shook his head. "Nope. I have already assigned someone incredible to deal with that matter."

"Then where are you… going?" Eva wondered what else could be so important for him to immediately leave again when they had just literally come back. She honestly even doubted if he had slept at all.

"I'm going back to finish our business. If I don't go back there now, they'll think we've backed out, and the Youngs will reap all the benefits that are supposed to be for ACEON. I can't possibly let your hard work go to waste just like that, can I?"

Eva's lips parted as she looked up at Gage. She never had expected him to go back to secure that project. She was not expecting him to…

She could not help the emotion that started to surge within her. But she bit her lip and tried her best not to show any of it.

"But… Gage… if you don't want to go and you want to stay with your grandfather, it's all right. If we lose that project, then… I suppose it can't be helped. I will just look for another bigger project. I will definitely find one." Eva

was going to be devastated to lose that deal as it was something that she was determined to have at all costs. It was a deal that would definitely cause a huge blow to XY, so Eva truly worked hard for it. But with Gage's grandfather being in this state, she could not be so selfish and heartless to have him leave his only family because of her desire to bring XY down.

Suddenly, he leaned over, surprising her at how close his face was to hers.

"I want to go, Eva," he said. "Grandfather is doing all right. And like I said, I would hate to let your hard work go to waste. You've pulled a lot of overtime for this. So I won't let the Youngs win, Eva. Not on my watch."

Eva bit the inside of her lip.

Sometimes, she really did not understand why this man was like this to her. She had been thinking since the beginning that it was all because he had some hidden agenda, but… what he was saying and doing right now was just… it was just…

She could not help but feel overwhelmed. She had never experienced this kind of support from anyone—such a willingness to go far beyond what was necessary to fulfill her best interests.

She was… she was used to fighting for things she wanted on her own… so all these were making her feel like…

He reached out and tucked a stray strand of her hair behind her ear and smiled gently at her. "So you just be a good girl and stay here. There is no need for you to worry about anything. Leave the rest to me, as you've already done your part. But before I go, why don't you give me a kiss, hmm… darling?"

And there it was again. That devilish, mischievous grin that never ceased to throw her off whatever state she was in.

Her gaze immediately fell to his lips, and she was instantly reminded of last night. Her face burned, but when she returned her eyes to his, the urge to just kiss him suddenly surged impossibly high within her.

She could not quite explain what she was feeling at that moment.

All she knew was that right now, she wanted to grant this man's request, whatever it may be.

Suddenly, he pinched her lightly on her cheek. His eyes gleamed with gentle amusement as he gazed at her.

"There you go again, being so serious," he uttered with a smile in his voice. "I changed my mind. I'll collect the kiss when I'm back instead. I'm afraid of the possible delay if you actually kiss me right now. Well then. I'd better get moving as I'm already going to be quite late."

His last line made Eva's eyes widen. That was right. How was he even going to make it to the project bidding in time?

"How are you going to make it in time?" she asked with genuine concern.

He gave her a smug smile.

"Don't worry, Eva, your man right here has his own secret, effective ways." He winked at her and then turned around to leave.

"W-wait… Gage!" she called out.

"Yes, darling?" he asked as he looked at her over his shoulder. A mischievous and suggestive smile slowly curled across his sexy lips.

Eva's breath stuttered a little as she saw it. He was making it hard for her to keep her mind straight and obediently say goodbye and send him off!

"Um… please be careful," she finally managed to say.

His smile grew wider.

"I will. Any other reminders before I really leave?"

"Um… be careful when you meet… Jessa. She might be planning something to… umm… Just don't allow her the chance to put her perfume on you again." Eva rapidly blinked as she felt her blood rush up her face, belatedly realizing that she was starting to sound somewhat like a jealous lover not wanting her man to be in contact with another woman. *Oh, gods… what in the world am I even saying?*

She was about to turn away and cover her burning face when he suddenly strode toward her with large, decisive steps. His eyes were devil-bright, and he looked ever so… happy as he wrapped both his hands around her wrists before pinning her against the wall, keeping her trapped between his long, powerful arms.

"I'll make sure to avoid her schemes. But… why don't you just mark your territory by kissing and biting me…

here?" He pointed at the side of his neck. "Just like what you did before, hmm? That will tell everyone that I'm off-limits."

Eva's jaw dropped. *W-what did he just say? My territory? H-him?*

"Of course… I am not forcing you to do it if the idea does not sit well with you," Gage whispered when Eva could not even give a response and just stood there, all red and flustered.

He stared at her flushed face for a few more moments and then chuckled in satisfaction.

"It's just a suggestion, Eva. Don't force yourself to do it."

He pinched her cheek lightly and added, "Rest assured, I will do my best to avoid catching that Jessa girl's scent on my person. See you, Eva darling."

Eva's heart stuttered while he was backing away from her.

Just as Gage turned to finally leave, she suddenly grabbed his hand. Eva pulled him back and pushed him against the wall.

And then, without wasting another second, she grabbed onto his collar, pulled him down, and raised onto her toes to lift herself up to meet him.

Her lips unceremoniously latched onto his neck, and she sucked hard at the thin and sensitive skin there.

When she finally pulled away, she stared at the spot she kissed marked with slightly narrowed eyes. Pleased, she drew in a deep breath and huffed in satisfaction, all the while nodding to herself.

"Still not satisfied with your work of art, darling?" Gage commented. "You are always welcome to try again. After all, the more, the merrier."

It did not take more than three seconds, and Eva's mouth was sucking on his skin again, this time much harder. She then moved her lips lower near his shoulder and bit him there. With the force that she had exerted, she was quite sure that there would be a ring mark from her perfect teeth on the skin of his neck.

"Damn, Eva…" His hands grabbed her shoulders, pushing her off him a little as he chuckled helplessly.

"But you said… the more the merrier?" she told him, still blushing hard, but her expression and the look in her eyes were incredibly serious. As if all that she did to him was pure, serious business! "And knowing Jessa… it is indeed much better if she sees more."

Somehow, Gage looked like he did not know whether to laugh or shake his head. In the end, he chuckled, running his fingers through his hair as he eyed her.

"I almost thought that you were trying to stop me from going." He sighed. "You're so not fair, darling. Attacking me boldly like that at the wrong place and the wrong time. That deserves punishment, and I can't wait to…" He trailed off and caught his lower lip between his teeth. "When did you even learn to behave this boldly, hmm?"

He pinched her chin and lifted her face.

"I'll look forward to your next attack, Eva. But next time, make sure we're in a private place. What you did just now is a little… dangerous." His thumb pressed on her lips and parted them. "Damn… I really need to go now… I'm already so late…" he murmured wistfully as his eyes kept darting back to her lips.

And then he bent and caught her earlobe between his teeth, causing Eva to freeze on the spot. "See you in a bit, darling," he whispered.

CHAPTER 32

"Gage mentioned to me what a workaholic you are… but I'm still honestly surprised, Miss Lee," the chairman commented, breaking the silence and causing Eva, who had been intensively reading documents from her tablet for a couple of hours now, to lift her head with a start.

"I'm so sorry. Do you need something, sir?" She immediately sprung from the couch and approached Gage's grandfather in his hospital bed. She was unsure if he had requested something from her as she was totally focused on reading the reports.

The chairman sighed softly.

"No, no… don't worry about it. I'm all good, young lady. But it's already quite late, and I wanted you to go have some rest now. You've been staring at your tablet for quite some time. The room next door is already prepared for your convenience, as Gage instructed someone to prepare it for you to stay in before you even arrived. So go on. Feel free to leave that tablet alone. You should be preparing for your beauty sleep," the chairman said good-naturedly as he lifted his hand and waved her off.

Eva just stood there, blinking at the elder.

Gage had been telling her to go to sleep since she started living with him, and she had already gotten used to it. Of course, she had never listened to Gage's words, but now that she had George saying this to her as well, it really surprised her.

Smiling, Eva respectfully shook her head. "I'm really fine, sir. I'm already used to working late into the night, and I don't think I can sleep even if I go to bed this early, anyway. So, I might as well continue with my work and be productive. Please don't worry about me as I have been like this ever since I was young. You know, I was pretty studious even when I was small."

George sighed, and Eva could not help but feel touched by the concern that flashed in his eyes. It was just so heartwarming that even an unrelated person like him could show her so much concern just because she was working a little later than normal working hours.

But his concern also brought a flash of bitterness as she thought of how the grandfather she grew up with had never shown such concern during those times when she slogged and worked her ass off to build XY into what it was today.

"You know, child… work and achievements are not everything. I am amazed and proud that you are such a hardworking and devoted lady. But…" George trailed off and smiled gently at her. "As someone older and who has seen life a little more, I would like you to take some time off for yourself, too. Find the time to relax and have fun. You are too young to overwork yourself like this. It's okay to slow down, Miss Lee. You might reach the peak you are after in no time, but if you get there by beating yourself up every day and night and never giving yourself a moment to breathe, you might not feel anything anymore once you have reached your aim. And wouldn't that defeat the whole purpose of getting to that peak in the first place?"

Eva could not respond to the advice that the chairman gave her. All she did was nod quietly. She wished that there was even one person in her so-called family who had shared one of these encouraging sentiments before. Even when she did not sleep, no one bothered telling her that it was okay to slow down. No one had asked her to take a break or stop and go to sleep early for her own sake. No one, not once.

"What are your hobbies, Miss Lee?" the elderly man asked, breaking the stilted silence between them.

Looking up at his kind eyes and warm smile, Eva knew that he was genuine in wanting to chat and get to know her more.

"Um… reading and…" Eva's eyes wandered. Now that she was asked, she realized that she did not have any hobbies. Well, maybe because she never had the time to find out about her interests? Her entire life was centered around studying and then, after graduating, working. She did not have the time to kick back, explore her interests, or do anything else but work. "I think I have yet to discover my hobbies if I still have any, sir."

He chuckled at how she answered, but his eyes looked at Eva with what may be called a fatherly concern.

"That is why you need to stop working once in a while. Don't bring your work home with you; simply do something else. Geez... what is that lazy grandson of mine doing?" George's voice started to sound annoyed. "Aren't you two already living together for weeks now? What is he so busy with that he's not doing anything to... He should've taken you out for dates so you could have fun! I'll definitely scold that lazy bum once he's back!"

Eva could not help cracking an awkward smile. "Actually, Gage is not lazy, sir. He's pretty amazing. Really! He shocks me every time he decides to show off his abilities."

"That's not going to excuse him. He should be doing something. Better yet, have a dinner date at night and then a whole weekend break for the both of you to just do your own thing and enjoy. That guy's pretty unromantic. I am starting to feel sorry for you."

"Er... um... actually, sir... Gage and I are—"

"Anyway, when will you two be getting married, Miss Lee? To be honest with you, young lady, I have been holding back from pressuring you two to get married because I was afraid I might destroy your relationship. I am very careful, because my grandson has finally found the woman he truly loves. But at this rate, I might really die without seeing my great-grandchild, and it's affecting my health."

George then sighed heavily while Eva just stood there, her lips slightly parted, completely stunned at the words the elder Acheron had spouted.

Gage… loves me? That is… that cannot be, right? Because why would Gage… no… there is just no way.

While Eva was busy denying and reasoning out things in her mind, a soft knock echoed through the room.

Eva whipped around and saw a tall, handsome, platinum blond-haired man entering the room.

"Grandpa…" his deep voice echoed as he went straight to the chairman's bed. "I'm glad you're not asleep yet."

"The audacity to actually come over this late, you punk!" the chairman scolded and pinched the skin between his brows while shaking his head at the handsome guy.

The guy lifted both his hands in surrender, seemingly hoping to appease George. "I'm sorry, okay? I've been caught up with a really big project, and it was already late when I heard the news. Besides, I knew you'd be fine. Gage, that guy, would not let anything happen to you anyway."

"Stop calling your brother 'that guy!'"

"Yes. Yes. Now, please, calm down, Grandpa. This is why I hesitated to visit. I knew I would only end up raising your blood pressure. Well, anyway." He shrugged nonchalantly before turning to look at Eva and eyed her from head to toe. A glint appeared in his gray eyes before he turned to question his grandfather. "Who is this hottie here, Grandpa? I hope she's not your sugar baby because if that's the case, I would really have a hard time accepting it."

"Don't you even dare lay your womanizing eyes on her, you brat! The lady already belongs to your brother," George warned, wagging his finger at the blond-haired man.

"Ah... how disappointing," he muttered under his breath before turning to face Eva again.

While the man was busy scrutinizing her, Eva's mind was flooding with many questions. She thought Gage was the only family the chairman had! But he actually had another brother? And his brother ended up being the current hottest movie star? Seriously?! Who would have thought?

"Stop staring at your soon-to-be sister-in-law, Hunter," the chairman's voice echoed warningly. "I'm not kidding."

"Geez, Grandpa! Ease up, will you? I am just admiring how beautiful she is. Can't I even do that? By the way, I'm Hunter." He extended his hand to Eva, a sexy, lopsided grin spreading across his lips.

Eva forced out a smile as she accepted his handshake. "Evelyn... Lee... it's a pleasure to meet you, Hunter."

"From what I've observed, it seems that Gage has never mentioned to you that he has a brother." He gestured to himself before leaning a little closer to Eva and whispered, "Well, it's supposed to be kept a secret. Because I am a famous superstar and Grandpa here… has disowned me because I chose to become an actor instead of running his company."

"Who the hell disowned you? You ran away from home and went to the extent of cutting ties with your family yourself, you punk!" the chairman bellowed at Hunter as he pointed an accusing finger at the young man, who was still grinning at her.

"Geez, Grandpa, stop spilling my embarrassing past in front of a hot lady," Hunter whined and complained playfully.

"I've warned you, haven't I? Don't even dare to trouble Miss Lee."

"But she's not Gage's wife yet, right? What if it's actually us who are fated to be together?" Hunter mischievously winked at his grandfather, who fell speechless for a few moments.

"You little… Miss Lee, you can go now and rest. Forget everything that this punk has said," the chairman spoke to Eva as if he would have probably already pushed and ushered her out of the room himself had he been able to stand.

"I… I understand. Please have a rest, too, sir." Eva nodded at the chairman before she lifted her gaze to Hunter. "And, sir, the chairman needs to rest. Please don't stress him out too much," she added strictly and then finally left.

CHAPTER 33

Eva was busy working in her room when a knock on her door disturbed her concentration.

That must be Hunter. Again!

Rolling her eyes, she only sighed to herself and looked at the door, making no move to get up to open it.

Hunter had been hanging around and taking every opportunity to bother her for the past two days, and he was becoming increasingly annoying.

Well, Eva was at least thankful because there was now someone seemingly trustworthy to keep company and watch over the chairman.

Though at first, she did not dare drop all her guard down just because Hunter was the chairman's other grandson, she eventually realized that the chairman was safe with Hunter. She could feel that the two were really fond of each other despite their constant bickering. She could also tell that Hunter genuinely cared about the chairman, from the patient way of enduring his

235

grandfather's nagging to the gentle smile he had on his face whenever the chairman was not looking.

However, whenever the chairman was resting or asleep, Hunter came and disturbed her.

Despite her ignoring all his antics, the bloody man was still unfazed. It was like he had super thick skin and did not know how to feel ashamed. He still came and bugged her, no matter how much she glared at him.

"Hi, Miss Lee." He sauntered into her room without even a by-your-leave and braced his arms shamelessly on her desk, flashing her a smile. "I have come to fetch you."

Eva frowned at him, not holding back her displeasure at him disrupting her work again.

"Grandpa asked me to take you out, Miss Evelyn. He told me to take you out for a… coffee break."

"Sure. We'll have a coffee break here, Hunter. I'll just order in. So there is no need for us to go out and waste all that time. What flavor do you want?" Eva asked straight up.

The man bit his lower lip and slowly released it, smiling. "So, it seems, even if with the chairman's favor, you'd still lovingly reject me like this, huh?" he murmured, his shoulders sagging as he half sat on her desk.

"I prefer to work over going anywhere outside, Hunter. There are tons of things that I need to get done, and going out would only derail my plans. Also, I am not in the habit of wasting and abusing the time that I am being paid to work." Eva's voice was clipped as her eyes looked sternly at Hunter.

He sighed loudly and dramatically, running his hand through his medium-length blonde hair. Once he removed his hand from his head, his hair fell forward, framing his face. "You're breaking my heart, Miss Lee," he said.

Eva narrowed her eyes at him. "I have something very important to finish right now. So, if you don't have any more important matters to convey, please leave my room," she politely but firmly told him.

"Ah, how cold…" He gave her an expression that made Eva quickly shut her eyes, and she reminded herself that this man was one of the best actors of his generation. He was actually the most expensive actor right now! She would do well not to be drawn in by his performance.

Not falling for his antics, Eva turned her attention back to her laptop and continued working, ignoring Hunter.

"By the way, Miss Lee… I've heard from my manager that you sent me a business email a week ago," Hunter said in a rather offhand tone, and almost immediately, Eva's fingers stopped flying over her laptop keyboard.

She looked up at him, and this time, she finally looked at him with interest, causing Hunter to smile.

"You ignored my email. May I know why?" Eva asked him with curiosity. "I figured you weren't interested, but now that I found out you're an Acheron, I can't help but wonder why you didn't respond at all."

Hunter tilted his head. "Well, let's just say that I was playing hard to get."

"So, you're just waiting for us to chase after you?"

"That's what the biggest stars would do, Miss Lee," he said proudly and confidently.

Eva almost rolled her eyes, but she refrained from doing so.

"But ACEON is your family's—"

"I know. I was just waiting for my dearest big brother to meet up with me or at least give me a call about the matter. But sadly, there was none." Hunter shrugged.

"It's because Gage was really busy this past week." Eva rose from her seat as she explained to him. She was the one who wanted Hunter to become their brand ambassador in the first place. Going through the long list of currently hot and potential male and female celebrities, she had narrowed it down to one and believed that this man was the perfect celebrity to represent the face of ACEON. Honestly, she was a little worried that he would end up choosing XY. So, she had truly put Hunter's name in the number one spot of celebrities they were considering. That was why, when he did not show even a little interest, Eva was really disappointed. And when she told Gage about this, Gage told her there was no need to contact Hunter again.

Eva thought that Gage must have been planning to call Hunter personally, but because of their busy schedule and their business trip, he must have forgotten to call his brother. Well, that was what she had wanted to think. But now that Hunter himself had mentioned it, Eva did not waste a moment more and went into the details, not giving Hunter any time to try to change the topic of conversation to something else.

Once Eva stopped talking, Hunter suddenly sighed and chuckled softly, looking at her with both amusement and disbelief. "I can't believe you'd only look at me and talk to me like this if I talk about business, Miss Lee."

"I'm only interested in business, Hunter," Eva answered him seriously, not a shadow of a smile on her face.

"Only... are you sure? So my brother is business to you as well, Miss Lee?"

Eva fell silent for a moment, but there was no change in her expression. His question had her mind almost reeling, but her mouth somehow opened, and she responded, "Gage is the only exception."

It was Hunter's turn to fall silent. He looked quite surprised while Eva tried her best not to blush at the words she had just blurted out without thinking. She could not believe she had said such words. But she knew in her heart that those words were the truth. Gage was... she hadn't thought of him as just some business transaction. He was the only man who could grab her full attention, even when he talked about the most mundane things.

"Wow... seems you're truly in love with my brother, Miss Lee."

Eva choked before coughing. She quickly went and poured herself a glass of water from the side table, all the while trying to compose herself. How did he come up with that conclusion?

Eva had actually been trying to be careful of her reactions to Hunter's words because of the strange thing the chairman had told her yesterday.

The chairman had told her to be careful of what she revealed to Hunter regarding anything related to Gage.

When she asked the chairman why, he told her something that felt kind of unsettling.

George had told her that Hunter was kidnapped when he was younger. And that it was Gage who found and saved him. But since then, George said that Hunter began to act a little off concerning anything related to his older brother and started to act a little obsessed with Gage. Hunter apparently suddenly wanted to know everything and anything about his brother, even down to the smallest detail, until it became unhealthy. George said that Gage never complained about it, but the chairman admitted that he was afraid Hunter might become nosy about Gage's relationship with Eva. And that was why George warned her and said that she could always choose to ignore Hunter and not say anything at all.

George also reassured her that Hunter was still a good child, apart from that one strange issue.

"All right, enough with the chit-chat. Let's get back to the topic of you being the face of ACEON," Eva shifted the conversation back to their business when Hunter looked away and fiddled with the plant on the side of Eva's table as though reluctant to let off their earlier topic.

"One last question, Miss Lee," he said slowly before he met Eva's eyes. Something in his gaze made Eva feel a little bothered. "Have you ever felt that something is… well… strange or… mysterious about Gage?"

A strange silence reigned between them.

Just as she opened her mouth to speak, her gaze caught a figure of someone leaning against the doorframe.

Eva sprung from her seat. "Gage!" she exclaimed, and then she rushed toward him. "Did you just arrive? How did everything go?"

Gage tilted his head and caressed her cheek with the backs of his fingers. His gaze seemed to search her thoroughly before his eyes finally landed on her own, which were locked onto him.

Smiling indulgently at her, he did not answer her question but asked his own. "You weren't being bullied here by Hunter while I'm not around, were you, darling?"

"Oh, come on, brother…" Hunter's voice echoed out from behind Eva. "Don't glare at me like I carried out some crime here. I do believe that it was Miss Lee who has been bullying me all this while. You might not believe it, but your secretary has completely ignored me for days! It's heartbreaking," Hunter pouted and complained to his older brother about the "injustice" he had received from Eva.

Eva whipped around toward Hunter, aghast at how blatantly he was spouting nonsense to Gage.

Wanting to defend herself, Eva retorted. "Hunter, I would appreciate it if you stop spouting such lies. I have always acknowledged you, even when you deliberately try to disrupt my work. So, do be mindful of how you word it. You can't simply say that I've completely ignored you."

"Still, Miss Lee... you have never even granted a simple request of mine to have coffee together. That is too much of a cold treatment that you are giving to your future brother-in-law, don't you think?"

Eva's lips parted but stayed hanging open and speechless at his accusatory words. She also could not believe how his facial expression was... *Oh, gods! This man was definitely using—and, in this case, misusing—his acting skills right now! And what did he just say? F-future ... brother-in-law?!*

"I believe you're just misunderstanding my darling here, Hunter." Gage suddenly stepped in and wrapped his strong and solid arm around her waist before pulling her back into his embrace. Leaning his chin on her shoulder, he nuzzled the side of her neck, causing Eva to freeze in an instant. "Miss Lee here has always been like that with everyone. She doesn't like to make small talk as it is a waste of her precious time. If you don't want to be ignored by her, talk about nothing but business. That's the way to go."

Eva saw how Hunter's eyes slightly widened at Gage's words. She honestly could relate because she herself was having almost the same response.

She had not expected him to... to defend her like that!

Hunter cleared his throat sheepishly before lifting his hand and rubbing the back of his neck.

"Well…"

"Well then, Hunter. Sorry, but I have to kick you out of the room this instant so my darling and I can… well, I know there is no need for me to spell it out for you. You get it, right?" Gage told him in a calm tone.

Hunter's lips parted. He looked like he could not quite believe what he was hearing from Gage's mouth. But he eventually smiled in disbelief and shook his head before pushing himself off the desk.

"Yes, yes." He lifted both hands in surrender before walking toward them. However, he stopped right before them and smiled at Eva. "I'm leaving for now. But we'll talk about that matter again next time, Miss Lee."

Eva could only nod. She was still taken aback by the excuse Gage had given his brother to get rid of him from her room.

Hunter grinned widely at her. But as soon as Hunter shifted his gaze to Gage, his smile turned taunting. He then walked past them but stopped and whispered to his brother, "Who would've thought that you're like this when you're in love… brother?"

Once the door was closed, Gage slowly moved away from Eva and made her face him. His gaze searched her once more.

"Hunter really didn't do or say anything weird to you, did he, Eva?" His previously teasing and lighthearted expression was completely gone and had suddenly become so serious.

She shook her head as she looked at him with a questioning gaze.

Gage sighed in relief.

"As promised, the project has been successfully dealt with." He smiled. "We got it."

Her eyes slowly widened. Her hands flew to cover her mouth in disbelief.

"I'm... oh, thank God! Thank you so much for making it happen, Gage! You're absolutely wonderful! The best!" she exclaimed, still gushing with her hands over her mouth.

"I made a promise, had I not? I would never make a promise to you that I won't be able to fulfill, darling," he murmured in a deep voice, causing Eva to blink and then blush a little.

"Now, my fiery little tigress"—he reached out and pinched her chin lightly before his smile turned into something... sexy—"I think it's high time for me to collect my just rewards."

Eva only realized that she was actually stepping back away from Gage when her back hit her desk.

She did not want Gage to think she was scared or trying to get away from her, um, responsibility, so she tipped her chin up to say something. But she was rendered speechless again at the sight of him smiling at her as if he were staring at something utterly adorable. Which she honestly thought was really puzzling because she knew she was nowhere near adorable. Her look was not what one would term adorable or cute. She had been told and had heard from various people countless times that she had a face that always looked angry at the entire world. She knew that was true, as she was aware of how rarely she smiled.

"I hope you're strategizing something exciting and intense in your head right now," he said, causing Eva to crease her brows at him.

"What… for?"

"Well… for my reward, of course! Don't tell me you've conveniently forgotten about it."

"I don't think there's any need for me to strategize anything for that."

"I believe otherwise, darling. Since, this time, I won't be accepting any of your punch kisses. After all, I do deserve some next-level reward, do I not?"

Her eyes turned a little intense as she replied, "Don't worry, Mr. Acheron. I'm not going to go for a punch-kiss, as you have called it."

His smile widened a little as he bent down, bracing his palms against the top of the desk, jailing her between his arms. "So, you already have a plan on how you'll devour me…"

What did he just say? Devour him?!

Pushing away from her, Gage suddenly walked away toward the door, leaving Eva speechless and lost as she stared at his retreating back.

Why is this man so unpredictable today?

Well, he was always unpredictable, but today, he seemed to be even worse!

When he reached for the doorknob and opened the door, Eva finally called out, "G-Gage?"

He looked over his shoulder and smiled at her. "Wait right here, Eva. I'll just go say hello to Grandpa first. After that, we can continue where we left off…"

After winking sexily at her, Gage closed the door behind him, leaving her staring mutely at the door.

CHAPTER 34

"You… reserved the entire restaurant?!" Eva's jaw dropped when she realized that the luxurious restaurant was empty except for the two of them. "Why would you…"

"Easy there, Eva. It's our first date. And I don't want you to keep acting as Evelyn Lee while you're on a date with me. So just be Eva, and let's enjoy the night together. Got it?"

Before Eva could respond, Gage had already guided her to a table by the floor-to-ceiling window, overlooking the beautiful, shimmering heart of the city. It was, without a doubt, the most scenic and romantic spot in the entire restaurant—a place most could only dream of sitting. The high ceiling was framed with ornate pillars and golden light fixtures, casting a warm glow that added a vintage elegance to the space. The lighting that bathed the room in just the right amount of illumination, created an intimate, cozy atmosphere without overpowering the gentle flicker of the candles in the center of their table.

Eva glanced around, still absorbing the sheer beauty and romantic feel of the place. "How did you even manage to reserve this place on such short notice?" she asked. This wasn't just any restaurant. It was the most exclusive, Michelin five-star establishment in Letran. Dining here was a privilege in itself, but securing *this* particular table in a short notice was said to be impossible. She'd never even had a chance to dine in this famed spot because it was always booked solid, with reservations made months, sometimes even a year, in advance.

She knew about all this because Julian once promised to take her here as a special date to make up for forgetting her birthday gift. She'd been looking forward to it back then, as she was also curious about this place. She had wanted to confirm if it was true that this very exclusive place was like no other, only for him to cancel, insisting it was impossible to book a table without personal connections to the owner. Julian had even brushed the place off as "overhyped," saying it was ridiculous to wait a year just for a dinner reservation. At the time, she'd shrugged it off and agreed. But now, experiencing it firsthand, she felt utterly enchanted. There was an undeniable magic here, a charm that seemed woven into every corner. She was certain now that this spot truly held the essence of the city's beauty and elegance in a way that no other place or spot could.

"Is the owner your grandpa's friend?" she asked, curiosity sparking in her eyes.

Gage chuckled. "No… actually, I'd say they have some beef with each other."

"What?" Eva's eyes widened. "Then how did you even… I heard it's impossible to book this place on short notice."

Gage shrugged, leaning closer as he held her gaze. "That's true, but…" He paused, a playful glint in his eyes. "If it's to impress you, I'll make the impossible possible." He grinned, and her jaw dropped.

Eva could only bite her lower lip. She could not quite explain the feeling that bloomed in her chest.

Clearing her throat, Eva reached out for the wine bottle. However, Gage swiftly grabbed it first and poured her a glass.

"Thank you," Eva murmured when Gage reached out and casually tucked a stray lock of her wavy red hair behind her ear.

"I've missed you," he uttered. "Did you miss me, hmm, darling?"

Eva's eyes flew back up to his. He was doing it again, flustering her badly with his words.

Her eyes wandered about, looking everywhere except into his eyes. She did not know what to say. She was not used to him talking so seriously. She honestly felt like she would prefer him to be mischievous and look at her with a teasing twinkle in his eyes, as always. This serious-faced Gage was… somehow, making her feel nervous and conscious.

"O-of course, I did," she finally managed to respond, not realizing that her tone almost sounded businesslike.

The corners of his lips lifted ever so slightly before he rested his head on his knuckles. "Really?" His voice held an inquiring tone as he arched one brow at her.

Looking away, Eva gave a slight cough before taking a couple of sips of wine from her glass. "A little..." she admitted reluctantly. He really had done so much for her. That project was truly something so important that she could not even begin to imagine how she should thank him. In fact, she could not even think of any reward that would be worthy enough to show him the full extent of her gratitude.

"I was... very occupied with work since you left. But I... I did miss you... a little," she added, her ears turning red. She was still unable to get used to being expressive about things like this.

His smile grew. "You seem unsure. How do you know you missed me, Eva?"

"I thought about you when... I went to bed. But it's not what you think! It's only because my phone alarm reminded me of something," Eva hurried to clarify.

"And?" Gage did not take his eyes off her even for a second, as if he did not want to miss every nuance of her expression.

She gently scratched the skin just below her ear. "And I... dreamed about you." The last few words were spoken so softly.

Gage sat up straighter.

"I'm guessing that the dream about me was not something nice, was it?" he asked.

Focusing on her steak, Eva replied casually, "Yes. It's not a good dream."

"Would you tell me about it?"

She met his gaze, hesitating before answering, "It's just... a weird dream."

Gage held her gaze silently, not pressing for details, yet his intense look made Eva glance away, suddenly finding her steak extremely interesting.

He sighed. "I hope I didn't scare you in your... weird dream."

She stopped cutting her steak, pondering for a moment. "I think you did... I mean, the 'you' in my dream did."

He leaned back, running his fingers through his dark hair as he chuckled with mock exasperation. "Now I really want to enter your dream and erase that damn little scary version of me. He shouldn't be ruining my reputation in your eyes and scaring you like that."

"Actually... you didn't do anything... bad to me or anything. You just... seem to disappear."

A brief silence passed.

"And that scared you...? Me, disappearing?" His voice was lower than usual as he asked that.

Eva nodded honestly to Gage before taking another sip of wine from her glass.

"I called out to you, but you didn't appear again. You were just suddenly gone, and I was left there all alone." She smiled awkwardly. "I know it's just a dream, but I did wonder what if you really don't come back."

He did not speak. He simply stared at her, his gaze deeper than ever.

"The thought made me feel a little scared."

She pressed her lips together. This felt really new, a little weird even. Because she was the type who always preferred to answer straight to the point and give direct and honest feedback. And she usually did not talk about things like this to anyone.

Never.

Reaching out, Gage poured more wine into her glass quietly.

And then he smiled, his eyes gleaming in the romantic light. He suddenly looked beyond pleased, causing Eva to frown and wonder what had made him look so happy.

She saw his expression dulled just a while ago when she mentioned her dream about him was not good. So what was with that ever-so-pleased look now?

As if he could read what was going on in her mind, Gage elegantly sipped on his wine and then said, "I'm happy because now I know you want me to stay with you forever, Eva."

Eva nearly choked on her mouthful of wine. Her lashes blinked furiously as she stared at him.

H-huh? But that is not what I...

He tilted his head, brows rising. "Aren't you scared to lose me, hm, darling? That only means that you want me to stay by your side forever, right?"

Her lips parted. Her color rose again. She cleared her throat and tried to gather her composure. "I think that's a little too… I was just afraid Jessa had succeeded in snaring you. Because once that happens, you'll turn your back on me as well and…" She trailed off when he reached out and put his hand on hers, stopping her from continuing. One side of his lips curled up as he took her hand in his.

"Come here, darling," he coaxed, his voice soft yet commanding as he gently pulled her closer, guiding her around the table until she was standing right in front of him. His touch was light, but his grip felt unbreakable, as though he had woven an invisible thread that pulled her into his orbit.

Eva couldn't help but ponder how this was even possible. Sometimes, she felt like a puppet in his hands, and Gage was the masterful puppeteer, skillfully pulling her strings with a mere word or look. He seemed to possess this uncanny power over her, an ability to make her move without thought, as though her actions were no longer her own. *Is this… even normal?* she wondered.

Why was it that, when it came to him, she found herself doing things she would never normally entertain with anyone else? She would never have thought herself capable of such compliance and quiet obedience. It was as if he had unlocked a side of her she didn't even know existed.

She had heard of people with such charisma, a magnetism so potent that they could sway others to do as they pleased, almost as if others were mere pawns in their hands. She thought he was simply one of those but as time passed, she was starting to think that there was still something different about Gage. She felt like his pull over her went beyond charm or simple persuasion. There was an intensity, a depth to his influence that felt both thrilling and unsettling. Sometimes he felt like an enigmatic force, one that seemed to blur her usual boundaries, leaving her wondering where her own will ended and his began.

"Jessa Young had indeed tried her best," he whispered as though they were sharing a secret. And those words effectively pulled Eva's wandering attention back to him. "Your warning was really on point. And even when I paraded your kiss mark, she barely cared about it and continued throwing herself at me. She's exactly as you warned me. Someone who'd do anything and everything to get what she wanted. And yes, she's pretty skilled. As much as I dislike admitting it, many men would foolishly fall for her smooth and calculated moves. But..." He suddenly tugged on her hand, and Eva was sent falling into his lap.

Eva whipped her head to face him, only to hold her breath at the realization of their faces' closeness. The sudden magnification of his seductive face so close caused her heartbeat to accelerate.

"I'm not among those foolish males, darling," he continued in a deep sexy voice. It was as though he had just stated a fact. "I am not dismissing your worries. I understand why you are worried now after I've seen for myself how Jessa Young carries out her antics. I think she won't stop even after how I treated her. Because she is the type who would never accept a blow to her ego."

Catching a lock of red hair between his fingers and playing around with it, something flashed across his beautiful eyes as he continued, "But let me make this clear—again. That woman doesn't hold a candle to you, Eva. Not even close. She could stand before me completely naked, and I'd still find you in your pink pajamas covered in little ducklings and bear prints infinitely more desirable. And, without a doubt, far sexier."

Her eyes stretched wide, utterly speechless. Her heart was tripping at the same time.

He chuckled so sensuously as he watched her dumbfounded expression. "Don't look like what I said is something utterly impossible, Eva. I will prove to you that every word I said is true."

She continued silently staring at him, searching his eyes with curiosity and wariness. And he simply let her do what she wanted. He did not disturb her scrutiny, which would probably be offensive or uncomfortable to others.

Until she finally opened her lips and spoke. "Why…" Her voice faltered a little before she swallowed and continued. "Why are you… being like this with me?"

There it was. Eva had said it. This was the same burning question that had been revolving within her mind ever since that day she woke up in his house. He had treated her with nothing but kindness, even going far beyond just simple kindness. Though he had been flustering her with his mischief, and despite the weird conditions in the contract that he came up with, Eva still could not figure out why this man was the way he was to her since the very beginning.

And though her initial deduction that he just needed a woman to show to his grandfather and settle his grandfather's worries truly made sense, especially now that she had seen how badly the chairman wanted his grandson to settle down, Eva still found that reason quite hard to believe. Just to have a fake girlfriend to appease his grandfather's worries, was it really necessary to go to such lengths and do all these things for her?

He tilted his head a little. His gaze was steady as he looked at her.

"Why…? Do I really need a reason to treat the woman I wish to marry well?"

Eva felt like steam was about to blow from her head. Her first reaction was to reach out with both hands and squeeze his cheeks between her palms. His reply was just something so hard for her to believe, so her brain told her he was not being serious again.

"P-please be serious," she stammered. "I'm being honest with you, so stop teasing me already and—"

His hands flew to her wrists and grabbed them gently but firmly. The look in his eyes had changed. She couldn't quite explain it, but this look was something he had never shown to her before.

"You should really stop thinking that I'm just teasing and playing around with you, Eva." There was no smile on his face nor mischievous glint in his eyes.

It took her a long while to respond. "Why… why me? Why do you want to marry me? Honestly, I've been wondering since the moment you asked me to marry you," Eva blurted out. "I have been wondering about your… your real motive… your hidden agenda…"

Worry then flashed in her eyes.

Her heartbeat drummed hard within her chest. Even though she neither felt nor saw anything worrying from him, even after what she had said, she still felt a trace of uneasiness. She could not help but worry that she might have gone too far with her words. What was with her tonight? She never thought that she would ever express those words to him, especially that last line! She should have omitted it!

"I…" She swallowed, faltering as her eyes wandered. She was nervous now about what the outcome of this would be. Her mind told her that this was definitely a risky conversation that could end something between them. And yet, she could not seem to stop herself from continuing, unable to hold back the words from tumbling out of her lips. "It's normal for me to think that way, right? Because…

it's really suspicious to me that you'd ask to marry a woman you have literally just met. And not to mention that I am… well, my current situation is certainly not a favorable choice for a man of your caliber. Yet you willingly helped me and treated me like I am someone… very special, and now you're even…" She finally bit her lips to stop the words from flowing out of her mouth.

She couldn't understand either why these things she normally found seemingly impossible to voice out before were strangely flowing so easily out now.

During his absence and after she had that dream, Eva had thought about a lot of things. She even thought of what would have happened to her if she had not met Gage that night. If she had not gotten drunk and somehow ended up in his home. Without Gage, she would probably still be somewhere, trying to stand again, perhaps even in another country. Because realistically, she would need years to get back on her feet. She had also thought of what would happen if Gage suddenly disappeared one day, too. If he turned his back on her like everyone else she had cared for in her life had done.

Just the mere thought of it had her experiencing an enormous feeling of fear she had never expected to feel. She was scared to be abandoned again.

To be thrown aside like she was some disposable, replaceable thing—just like what her so-called family and fiancé had done to her. Though she had survived it once, she had a nagging feeling that she might not survive it easily if Gage turned his back on her and left her.

But Gage returned. And he did not just return to her. He came back with such incredible news. And now, he was holding her and telling her such unbelievable things.

She had wanted to think that maybe she had finally found her very own good luck charm—him. Gage Acheron. A mischievous and mysterious male who had seemingly offered to marry her on a whim, a dethroned stranger he just met.

She had also considered that perhaps he had experienced what people often say was love at first sight. But Eva immediately shook her head frantically at that frivolous thought. Such a thing was just too surreal. It was just too impossible for her to believe.

"You're right, Eva," he finally replied. "It's normal and not surprising that you would think that way. You're not a naive woman, and I know you consider things very thoroughly." A gentle smile curved across his handsome face, making Eva feel instantly relieved.

The fear and the thudding in her heart mellowed out. She felt utterly thankful that he wasn't reacting negatively to her words.

"I understand if you find my words and actions toward you unbelievable," he continued. "It's understandable that you are now being overly cautious and wary of anyone and everyone's motives toward you because of those idiots who had betrayed and cast you away. All I can say is their loss is my gain!" A devilish grin spread across that handsome face that never ceased to dismantle her composure.

When his grin faded, that rare and serious look returned. His eyes turned darker than ever. Gage lifted his hand and caressed her cheek with the backs of his fingers. "As for your main concern"—a breathtaking gleam flashed across his dark eyes as he spoke—"I proposed to marry you because I want you."

A long stretch of silence reigned as they just stared into each other's eyes. Eva, still gauging and thinking through his words, while Gage patiently waited. It looked like he was absolutely telling the truth.

However, despite it all, Eva still could not hide the doubt and disbelief that was on her face. Despite how her heart reacted to his words and the seemingly sincere look in his eyes, her mind was too guarded and doubtful to fully accept and believe.

"No complicated motives or any hidden agendas?" she asked nervously before chuckling a little sheepishly. She knew that there was a chance he might end up being offended by her disbelief even after expressing himself so honestly and sincerely to her.

Gage did not respond to that statement. He simply stared deep into her eyes.

Then he rose. Taking his glass of wine with him, Gage stood by the window and stared at the bright city below.

His actions had Eva's heartbeat race a little harder. But she followed him and stood by his side, looking down at the beautiful view. She had to admit that whatever he was planning, this place he had brought her to was truly top of the line. There was nothing to criticize about the place, its scrumptious food, the intimate and romantic ambiance, and the fantastic view. They were all perfect—just as he was perfect, too.

He turned and leaned his back against the glass, his gaze now focused on her face. "I think it's useless if I answer that question of yours right now," he said in his usual deep and velvety voice. There was no sign that he was offended or annoyed. "No matter the answer, you'd still doubt it. But I understand why you're being like this, too."

Reaching out, he pinched her chin lightly with a fond smile gracing his lips. "I knew it would take time for you to drop your guard and trust my words fully, darling," he whispered into her ear, sending a ticklish sensation running down her back. "Worry not, Eva, I'm not going to rush you. I can wait forever if the reward is you."

The glass fell from her listless fingers and shattered at her feet, shocking her. His words totally made her forget about everything else, even the fact that she was holding a glass of wine!

Damn it...

"Don't move." His firm voice echoed, and when he moved to scoop her into his arms, Eva lifted her hand to stop him. She was wearing heels. There was no need for him to carry her because there was no way she would get hurt. All she had to do was step away from the glass shards.

But he still caught her wrist and flashed her that breath-stealing smile.

"Let me do this for you, darling."

Before she could say anything further, he scooped her up in a flourish.

"Was what I said really that shocking?" He chuckled throatily as he just stood there with her in his arms.

Blushing, Eva cleared her throat and tried to regain her composure. "Are… you sure about what you just said? Or did you forget that you have given me only a month to decide whether to marry you or not?"

There was a short pause before his sensuous chuckle echoed around them again. "Well"—he sighed, his expression turning neutral—"marrying you and having you are two very different things. Isn't that right, Eva? I can wait for eternity if the reward is having all of you—heart, body, and soul. But… I cannot wait that long to marry you."

Eva's lips parted and remained that way for a while.

"I can wait forever if the reward is having all of you— body, heart, and soul…" Those words echoed in her head again and again.

My God! Are all these happenings real? I should not be dreaming with my eyes wide open, right? Is Gage really sober right now? At this rate, he is… he is going to…

It took her a moment longer to manage a sentence again. "Why? Is there a reason why marrying me can't wait? Is it… because of the chairman?"

"Hmm… he's one of the reasons," he replied with a small nod.

"Then what… are the other reasons?" Curiosity made the lines between her brows reappear.

"Nothing complicated, darling," he replied. "I just want to mark you as mine and as soon as possible before anyone else dares to snatch you away. Not that I'd politely stand aside and let anyone even dare try to take my woman…" Gage trailed off. Whatever he saw in her expression caused a slow, devastating smile to flash across his face.

Eva belatedly noticed she was not breathing well. In fact, she must have forgotten how to breathe for a few moments there. *This man is truly bad for my health!*

"W-who would even… want to snatch me away? People do the opposite to me." She faked a breathy laugh. "And I don't think… that I am your… w-woman, Gage. We're not even in a… relationship."

Putting her down, he cupped her face. Gage's eyes seemed to burn with a dark fire that sent something hot skittering all over her skin. "That's something we're going to have fixed very soon, Eva." His smoky voice held a confidence that could be perceived as arrogance.

But God help her, because even his attitude right now was not alarming her. It seemed to be seducing her instead. "You'll officially be my woman very soon, Eva."

CHAPTER 35

The instant Eva woke up, she sprung up in a panic to look at her side table. And when she noticed that her alarm had been turned off and she was already very late, she just sat there, frozen, for a while.

But after going through the stages of grief in a span of a few minutes, she finally moved and climbed off her bed.

She rushed into Gage's room only to find that he was no longer there. He was, in fact, not in the house anymore.

Soon, she was seated in her car, heading to work. She could not believe that Gage did not bother to wake her up. What was worse, he had even turned off her alarm!

Last night, their date was fun. After their dinner, he allowed her to enjoy herself drinking instead of reminding her not to drink too much like he usually does. He did not even ask her for any kisses like she had been expecting him to do, but just let her relax, drink, and get drunk.

Her memories were a little blurry, but she knew that she had only talked and spouted gibberish the entire time after their serious talk while Gage watched her, occasionally laughing at what she said. And then she remembered him carrying her on his back as they left that luxurious restaurant.

The next thing she remembered was her being gently laid on the bed. To her embarrassment, she also remembered herself clinging on to him and repeatedly asking him to kiss her. She did not remember anything after that, but Eva somehow knew that Gage must not have given in to her. She just knew. Because Gage would not do anything to her if she did not have her wits about her enough to understand what she was doing.

CHAPTER 36

Upon arriving at the office, Eva found Gage seated at the CEO's desk, busily dealing with someone on the phone while reading and signing a document that was open in front of him.

Gods... He is even hotter when he is focused like that! Truly, men look their handsomest when they are fully concentrating on their work!

As though sensing someone's gaze on him, Gage lifted his head, and upon seeing her, his dark eyes twinkled. That previously strict and serious look on his face had softened dramatically with the lightening of his eyes.

Eva settled her things on her desk and then went to make Gage his favorite cup of coffee.

When she got back, she overheard what Gage said over the phone while his chair was turned around and facing the window.

"Yes. The evidence should be there... I need everything to be ready as soon as possible... All right."

When he ended the call, he swiveled around in his chair and smiled at Eva.

"I wasn't expecting you to be here so soon, darling. You should've rested a bit more."

"You turned my alarm off again," Eva said a little accusingly as she placed his coffee on the desk.

"I just wanted you to rest, and I assumed by how drunk you were last night, you might be nursing a hangover. Are you okay, hm, darling?" He stood up, walked around his desk, and reached out to feel her forehead.

Eva could only bite on her lower lip and look up at him, her cheeks a little hot at how intimate they might look at this moment.

"I'm fine..." she answered a little shyly before she immediately regained her composure and stared at him with a serious gaze. "You came to work so early. Did... something happen?"

"Ah... now this must be the negative of me being tardy all the time." He chuckled, looking amused. "Nope... nothing serious, Eva. In fact, it is just the normal daily things that need to be attended to."

"Oh... I see..." Her gaze then fell to the desk, staring at the folders pile. "You've finished a lot already. It's like you've been here since last night."

She narrowed her gaze at him, trying to read through his nonchalance.

"Well... I guess I'm a bit fired up." He then flashed her a grin.

She tilted her head a little, wondering what it was that had gotten him so excited. "Why?"

"Because the investigation into your case is going really well. I didn't think that Mr. Young was that careless. We've easily found the evidence that will put your name in the clear and that you were nothing but the Youngs' scapegoat."

Eva could not speak. She could only stare up at him, not knowing what to say.

"Don't worry about it, Eva. I assure you they will—"

"I'm not worried about them at all, Gage," she broke off, and then a soft, small smile tugged at the corner of her lips. "To be honest, I'm worried about something completely different right now."

His eyebrows furrowed. "Tell me… what are you worrying about, hmm?" His voice was low and magnetic as he said that.

"I'm a little worried about the fact that I'm not worried at all. I think… I'm already trusting in you way too much, depending and relying on you way too much, and… I…" She trailed off when Gage suddenly pulled her against him.

He half sat on the desk and had her sandwiched between his legs, pressing her face against his chest.

"I know you've always been an independent woman your whole life, Eva," he began, "and I believe, right now, you want to fight your enemies and take them down with your own abilities. With your own power. If you had any other choice, I know you would definitely turn down all my help because you would want to do it without anyone's help. I do understand why you'd rather want that because it would most probably be more fulfilling, but..." He trailed off and sighed before he held her shoulders and made her look at him. "But, darling... it's okay to get some help. You've been by yourself for so long already, relying on no one but yourself. Don't you think it's about time for you to wholeheartedly accept someone else's help and just rely on them too?"

The way he stared at her intensely as he spoke those words made Eva feel like words had failed her once again. Those words... he had no idea how strong they were striking right into her heart.

"Besides..." he continued, his expression changing into something soft yet a little wicked, "they haven't been playing fair when dealing with you in the first place. It's been one person against many all this while. Though what they did only shows how strong you are and that they needed to come at you all at once, I still think it's about time for you not to be a lone wolf anymore. You don't have to do it by yourself, and you can now learn to get more and more comfortable receiving assistance from me. Accepting someone's helping hand never means failure or weakness, Eva... You know that, right?"

Their gazes held for what felt like a very long time until Eva let out a shaky breath and then nodded slowly.

"I know, Gage..." she replied softly, and he smiled, caressing her cheek with the backs of his fingers.

"Good girl…" he murmured. "Don't worry, I will make sure not to overdo it. You'll still be the one who will do most of the work on this matter. I am merely a supporting role right behind you. Now, darling, it's time for you to take a seat and work on this… I believe this will set you on fire." He winked at her as he placed a folder in her hands.

CHAPTER 37

Just as Gage had said, Eva had been a fiery working machine the entire day.

Everything else had been set aside from her mind and forgotten for the time being. What was left was only work and more work.

She had worked overtime, and Gage did not bother to say anything. He had not nagged her to stop working or to take a break. Since she had arrived late to work, she was making up for it with overtime now.

And before she knew it, the clock had already struck midnight. Groaning, she realized that she had forgotten to reset her alarms!

Frantically rising from her desk to look for Gage, Eva was surprised to see that he had fallen asleep on the couch in their office.

When she woke up the next morning, she was lying on the bed in the private room in the CEO's office.

And again, Gage was gone.

271

That day, Eva traveled to Gage's place for an emergency matter they had to deal with in their New York branch.

Gage had another important meeting to attend that he could not miss, so Eva suggested that she address the other matter by herself instead.

Gage had been a little hesitant, and she somehow felt he had wanted to object, but in the end, he still gave in.

And thus, Eva had gone ahead for her very first solo business trip without Gage.

CHAPTER 38

After another long and taxing day, Eva was finally back in her hotel room. She was finally going back tomorrow. Everything was wrapped up and done, and it had been such a success that she was still unable to keep herself from smiling.

It had been so long since she felt this kind of adrenaline rush, and all she wanted right now was to share the good news with Gage.

He was the first and only one in her mind the moment the issue was successfully resolved.

Tossing and turning around in bed, Eva grabbed her phone. She kept debating if she should just call him. But then, she wanted to tell him the news in person.

In the end, she put her phone down on the side table. She then forced herself to sleep. But unfortunately, sleep was not coming to her.

All because… because she just could not stop thinking about him… about Gage. No matter how she tried, he seemed to be so firmly stuck in her head that even in her sleep, she began to dream about him.

Last night, she slept only a few hours for the same reason. Him. She kept wondering why Gage did not ask for his kisses as he usually did. Even when she left for this business the other day, he had not taken the opportunity to flirt with her and ask for any goodbye kisses.

Eva knew that they had been very busy since the day after their date. But she also knew that before this, no matter how busy they both were, Gage would always find time to flirt and ask for a kiss. In fact, she had honestly been waiting for him to bring up the reward they talked about back in the hospital that day, but it was as if he had completely forgotten it.

It had been days since they last kissed. Though the circumstances seemed to be just coincidental, which had led to them being unable to do so, Eva kept feeling like something was off.

She had only known Gage for a short time, but she knew that if he wanted to, he would always find a way to have his kisses no matter what. So why? Why did he not ask for her kisses before she left? Was she just overthinking this again? Or was she just... missing him? Missing his kisses?

Burying her face in her pillow, Eva took a few deep breaths and began to talk herself out of it. She should stop overthinking and just go to sleep. She tried convincing herself that she would be seeing him very soon tomorrow anyway.

Just as she was about to fall asleep, her phone vibrated.

She sprung from her bed and grabbed it, only to crease her brows at the sight of Hunter's name flashing on her screen.

Now, what is this? Why is this annoying little brother of Gage calling in the middle of the night?

Deep within her, she'd been wishing it was Gage who called. Hence, she couldn't deny her disappointment when she saw Hunter's name instead.

After thinking for a moment, she answered the call.

"Sister-in-law! Good evening!" Hunter's voice echoed loudly in the dead silence of the night, so much so that Eva pulled her phone away from her ear, grimacing at the loudness of his greeting.

"It's almost midnight, Hunter. What can I do for you?" she replied, all prim and proper and businesslike.

"Yet you're still awake? Working overtime again, I'm sure. You should really stop working late, Miss Lee. Sleep does wonders for your skin, you know—"

"I'm going to sleep now—" Eva cut him off.

"Wait a minute!" he yelled and then sighed heavily. "Can't you at least give me some time to beat around the bush?"

"It's midnight. And if you don't have anything important to say—"

"All right, all right! Well, I have some news for you… I believe you haven't seen this yet. Knowing you, you would not even have caught any gossip about it yet."

"Please get to the point, Hunter."

"Fine, I'm sending it to you now so you can see it for yourself. But wait… you will owe me dinner for this one, okay?"

Creasing her brows, Eva considered it. She couldn't believe he was going to negotiate with her in the middle of the night like this!

"Oh, come on, sis-in-law! Just say yes. This is BIG news! I swear this will rock your world!" Hunter nagged.

"Fine, fine. Just once!" She finally gave in as she was utterly curious about what this man was talking about.

"Perfect! Okay, here you go. And oh, do prepare your heart before checking it." Hunter threw out those last words before ending his call.

After a breath, her phone beeped. And for some reason, she found herself feeling a little… uneasy.

Eva's finger hesitated for a moment before she tapped on the message.

And what she saw next had her entire body going utterly still.

It was a photo of Gage and Jessa caught in an intimate angle with a headline: "The CEOs of rival companies XY and ACEON are hooking up!"

For what felt like a very long time, Eva just stared at the screen of her phone, not making a single movement or any sound. She just continued staring down at that photo, at that headline.

Slowly, she moved from the bed and rose. Gripping her phone in her hand, which was stiff by her side, she walked toward the floor-to-ceiling windows and stared down at the buzzing city nightlife. Her gaze was staring unseeingly into space.

Another long while passed before she made any move again. Lifting her free hand, she absentmindedly touched the glass. And then her fist slowly clenched against it.

She lifted her phone and made a call. "I'm leaving. Right now…" she said in a neutral voice the moment the call was connected. "I have changed my mind. I'm taking Gage's private jet. Also, don't tell anyone I'm headed back home tonight. Not even Gage."

CHAPTER 39

It was dawn when Eva finally arrived at Gage's mansion.

She stopped by the massive doors and stood there in silence for a couple of minutes. Now that she was here, she found herself chickening out. A part of her was telling her she did not have the right to do this. Gage was... he was not hers to begin with. What they had between them was a contractual arrangement.

However, the other part of her aggressively ordered her to lift her chin up and march right in with guns blazing and demanding answers. This more daring side was telling her that though Gage was indeed not officially hers, the two of them had an agreement. And he... he even gave her his word not once, but twice.

Eva's mind was in total chaos. This just reminded her so much of that wretched night in Julian's apartment. And she could not deny the existence of the fear that was creeping under her skin.

She was scared to find out that... the news was true.

What would she do if the news was true? What would happen to her from here on if… if…

Clenching her fists and biting on her lower lip so hard that she could taste the metallic tang of blood on the inner surface of her lips, Eva expelled a sharp, deep breath.

Her body managed to relax, but her gaze boring at the door handle became even fiercer. It was pointless for her to still be standing out here and asking herself countless questions that could only be answered by entering the house and meeting with said person in question. She was always the type who would bravely confront someone when she needed answers and when she had the chance, no matter how nerve-racking it may be. Therefore, today's incident should be no different from any other time.

Pushing the door open, Eva tried to ignore the insanely loud thumping of her heart. She entered quietly but confidently, her head held high and her eyes bright and alert.

The living area was quiet. Empty.

Almost all of the lights were turned off. But that was nothing unusual since it was dawn, and it was the norm in this house. But… was it just her mood that had made the place look a bit… Eva could not quite express in words what it was that had her on edge, but she felt like something was off.

She chose to shake her head in the end and locked the door behind her, telling herself to ignore the weird sense she had as it might just be her feeling slightly nervous.

Glancing at the fireplace where Gage usually loved to lounge around, Eva's hold on her bag tightened.

She ascended the stairs and surprisingly, right at this moment, she felt as if she was at her calmest. She had thought her emotions were going to get the better of her the moment she was here.

But here she was. Save for her loud and fast heartbeat, she was much calmer than she had ever thought she would be. This feeling somehow gave her a twinkle of hope, hope that whatever answer she got once she opened the door to his room would not be something that would break her heart.

Lifting her right hand and forming a fist, Eva knocked softly on his door and listened for a response.

Silence was the only thing she got.

Creasing her brows, she knocked again—a little louder this time. And when there was still no answer, she pushed at the door.

The room was pitch-black, and there was no sign of him being in his room.

Still, Eva reached out for the switch and turned the lights on.

His bed was perfectly made. Everything was flawlessly in place. And Gage himself was not here.

Eva's heart sank, and all she could do for a long stretch of time was to stand there, staring blankly at his bed.

Gage was not fond of sleeping just anywhere, even in hotels or in his office. She had also heard from the butler that if Gage was not out of the country, he would never stay away the entire night and always come home and sleep in his house no matter how late. Gage himself confirmed it when she asked.

Yet he was not here, and it was almost daybreak.

Closing his door, Eva did not immediately head to her room but instead chose to walk down the stairs again, rather absentmindedly.

She did not like all these feelings that were making themselves known in her heart. Since the moment she saw that news… strong emotions she never thought she had in her were now rearing their heads, threatening to overwhelm her. This was all so different from what she felt that night in Julian's apartment.

If the news was true, and that was why Gage was not here… it would only mean that… Gage had betrayed her, too. Just like Julian did.

But her rage did not blaze like how it did with Julian. The feelings she was experiencing now were totally foreign, and she hated them because she did not know how to deal with them. She did not even know how to express how she was feeling and get it out of her system.

Raging was… easier than this.

Standing by the cold fireplace next to Gage's favorite chair, Eva wondered if these feelings were signs of her impending doom. Were all these… was everything about to crumble down once again?

She shook her head.

I must trust Gage. He is different. That news… it must just be Jessa's antics again.

Right. Gage is not like Julian.

But… what if… what if Jessa had succeeded? What if she found Gage's weakness, which caused him to finally fall for her trap?

No matter how much she tried to tell herself that Gage was different, that he was no fool, Eva realized that she simply couldn't fully trust him anymore. It was no longer that easy. And that truth made her throat ache, but what could she do?

The sudden booming clap of thunder jolted Eva out of her thoughts.

She whipped her head toward the open garden and was surprised that it was actually raining hard now.

As her eyes focused, Eva's brows furrowed. Something… no, someone was outside in the rain.

Her heart stopped for a moment.

"Gage?" she whispered, unsure.

Her feet moved closer toward the open garden.

Suddenly, another bolt of lightning cut through the darkness, and Eva caught a glimpse of a man's silhouette— a silhouette that she was certain belonged to Gage. But that wasn't the only thing she saw in that brief, shocking moment. She also saw something impossible—a massive, looming shape that seemed to stretch out behind him like wings.

THE STORY CONTINUES IN

I MADE A DEAL WITH THE DEVIL

Volume II

KAZ ZEN

ACKNOWLEDGMENTS

I would like to extend my utmost gratitude to all my readers. I love you all and thank you so much for your support. You have made my dream come true.

To Chi, the special friend who has been my greatest support since the beginning of my writing journey, I love you, and I could never thank you enough.

To Edi, Basia, and Michelle, my amazing friends who have gone above and beyond to show their support for me, thank you from the very bottom of my heart. No words are enough to express how grateful I am that you never tire of being there for me, always willing to do anything for me, no matter what.

To Bobbi, Helen, Patty, Susan, Monica, Despina, and Rose, thank you always. I will never forget the immense support you once gave me.

To Dreamer, April, Dani, Lois, Jennifer, and everyone on Patreon, thank you so very much for your never-ending support. You guys rock!

And of course, to Gisel, you are the best!

ABOUT THE AUTHOR

Kazzen is a romance fantasy writer best known as the author and scriptwriter of the comics I Made a Deal with the Devil and His Duchess is a Ghost. She loves books, dogs, and coffee.

Made in the USA
Middletown, DE
28 December 2024